"Where do we start?"

Gavin glanced over at Layla. "We can start by talking about us."

He could tell from her expression that she didn't think that was what they should be talking about.

"We agreed to discuss the dig and not this thing between us," she said.

Gavin wondered if Layla knew that "this thing" actually had a name. It was called *desire*. "I think we should talk about us before discussing the dig."

She gave him an annoyed look. "Why? I told you last night we need to keep sex out of it."

Yes, she had said that, but did she actually think they could when there was so much sexual chemistry between them?

"I want you and you want me."

"And?"

Maybe it was time to explain what he meant. "And…" he said, "we *will* sleep together."

The Rancher Returns

BRENDA JACKSON

MILLS & BOON

First published in Great Britain 2016
By Mills & Boon, an imprint of HarperCollins*Publishers*
1 London Bridge Street, London, SE1 9GF

Large Print edition 2016

© 2016 Brenda Streater Jackson

ISBN: 978-0-263-06643-2

Our policy is to use papers that are natural, renewable and recyclable products and made from wood grown in sustainable forests. The logging and manufacturing processes conform to the legal environmental regulations of the country of origin.

Printed and bound in Great Britain
by CPI Antony Rowe, Chippenham, Wiltshire

Brenda Jackson is a *New York Times* bestselling author of more than one hundred romance titles. Brenda lives in Jacksonville, Florida, and divides her time between family, writing and travelling.

Email Brenda at authorbrendajackson@gmail.com or visit her on her website at brendajackson.net.

To the love of my life, Gerald Jackson, Sr.
My first. My last. My everything.

To everyone who loves the
Westmorelands, this book is for you!

To the 1971 class of William M. Raines
High School, Jacksonville, Florida.
Best wishes on our 45th class reunion.
Ichiban!

Plans fail for lack of counsel,
but with many advisers they succeed.
—*Proverbs* 15:22

Prologue

"Hey, Viper, your cell phone was going off upstairs."

Gavin Blake, known to his SEAL teammates as Viper, nodded as he set his coffee mug on a side table in the barracks' common area. Standing, he stretched the kinks out of his body and felt his aches all the way to the bone. Their last covert operation had been risky as hell, but they'd succeeded in destroying yet another ISIS stronghold.

In two days they would officially be off duty and most of his teammates would be heading for home. However he had other plans. Getting laid was at the top of his agenda. It had been too long since he'd shared a woman's bed and he'd already made plans with a beautiful bartender he'd met in Mississippi while helping his teammate Bane out of a fairly dangerous situation several months ago.

Gavin raced up the stairs toward his berthing unit and retrieved his cell phone from the gear in his bunk. He'd missed a call from Sherman Lott, the man who'd lived on the neighboring ranch for years. Panic floated through Gavin's belly. Had something happened to his grandmother?

Since his grandmother lived alone when he was away, Gavin had given their closest neighbors his contact information in case of emergencies. Of course the foreman was there, running the ranch in Gavin's absence. Surely if something was going on with his grandmother, Caldwell would have contacted Gavin. But what if this was one of those times when Caldwell had gone to Saint Louis to meet with one of their beef distributors?

Gavin quickly pressed the redial button and Mr. Lott picked up on the second ring. "Hello?"

"Mr. Lott, this is Gavin. Has something happened to Gramma Mel?"

"No, Gavin, your grandmother is fine physically. Not sure what's happening to her mind, though."

Gavin frowned, wondering what the man meant. Although she was nearing her seventy-fifth birthday, Gavin had never known a day in all his thirty-two years when Melody Blake hadn't been sharp as a tack. He'd spoken with his grandmother two weeks ago and she had sounded just fine to him. "What makes you think something is wrong with her mind?"

"She's allowed some fast-talking college professor to convince her that the outlaw Jesse James buried some of his loot on the Silver Spurs, and they plan to start digging up parts of her land next week."

Gavin refrained from correcting the man. The land was *their* property since Gavin legally owned all eight hundred acres jointly with his grandmother. Instead he concentrated on what Lott had said. His grandmother had given someone permission to dig on the Silver Spurs?

"There must be some mistake, Mr. Lott. You know my grandmother as well as I do. There's no way she would allow some man to—"

"It's a woman. A professor by the name of Dr. Harris."

Gavin drew in a deep breath. Who the hell was Dr. Harris and how had she talked his grandmother into agreeing to a dig on Blake land?

Rubbing a hand down his face, Gavin knew he would be flying home and not making that pit stop in Mississippi after all. *Damn!*

"Gavin?"

"Yes, Mr. Lott, I'm here."

"I hated to call you knowing you're probably somewhere doing important work for our country, but I felt you needed to know what's going on."

"And I appreciate you doing so. Don't worry about a thing. I'll be home in a couple of days."

Gavin hung up the phone and cursed in anger. He then placed a call to his ranch foreman, Caldwell Andrews. The phone was answered on the third ring.

"Caldwell? What's going on at the Silver Spurs? Sherman Lott just called and he thinks Gramma Melody has gone loco. He said something about her allowing some professor to dig on the ranch?"

He heard Caldwell curse under his breath

before saying, "I wish Lott hadn't called you, Gavin. Your grandmother is fine. She likes the professor. They talked and according to Ms. Mel she read the professor's report and it's legit."

Viper rolled his eyes. "Caldwell, you know as well as I do that there's no buried treasure on the Silver Spurs. If you recall, when I was in my teens, Dad allowed this outfit to come in and dig up parts of the land when they convinced him there was oil somewhere on it. Not a drop of oil was found."

"I remember. But I guess Ms. Mel figured a little digging wouldn't hurt anything since it's a small area, away from the main house and far away from where the cows are kept. It's the south pasture."

"The south pasture?"

"Yes. Nobody ever goes over there."

Nobody but me, Gavin thought. He knew everyone thought of the south pasture as wasted land since it had compacted soil, little or no vegetation and unsuitable irrigation. However, that part of the ranch was where he could escape and find solace whenever he needed to be alone. For some reason, going there always renewed his spirits. It was where he'd gone as a kid whenever he would miss his mother, where he'd gone after getting word about his father being killed in the Middle East. And last year he had camped out there a couple of days after returning from his mission and believing his teammate Coop was dead. It was there in the south pasture where Gavin had dealt with the thought of his good friend dying.

"Like I said, Gavin. Your grandmother has everything under control."

He wasn't so sure of that. "I'll find that out for myself since I'll be home in a few days. Don't mention my visit to Gramma Mel. I want to surprise her." When he hung up the phone, he rubbed a frustrated hand down his face.

"Viper? Hey, man, you okay?"

Viper turned to see four sets of eyes staring at him with concern. His SEAL teammates. They were Brisbane Westmoreland, team name Bane; Thurston McRoy, team name Mac; Laramie Cooper, team name Coop; and David Holloway, team name Flipper. The five of them had survived all phases of SEAL training together and were not only teammates, but like brothers. More than once they'd risked their lives for each other and would continue to have each other's backs, on duty or off.

"Viper?"

He heard the impatience in Mac's voice and spoke up before Mac's edginess got the best of them. "It's my grandmother."

"What about Gramma Mel?" Flipper asked, moving closer. Each of them had at one time or another gone home with Viper and met his grandmother.

"Is she sick?" Bane asked.

Viper shook his head. "No, it's nothing like that. My neighbor called to let me know that Gramma Mel gave some college professor permission to dig on our property. This professor has convinced my grandmother that Jesse James buried some of his stolen loot on the Silver Spurs."

The worried expressions on his friends' faces switched to relief and then amusement. "Is that all?" Coop asked, grinning, resting his broad shoulder against a wall.

"That's enough. Nobody has permission to dig on the Silver Spurs."

"Evidently your grandmother gave it," Bane pointed out.

"Well, that permission is being rescinded, and I'm going to make sure Gramma Mel and this professor know it."

"Did you talk to Caldwell?" Flipper asked.

"Yes, but he'll go along with anything my grandmother says. Now I have to head straight home instead of making that pit stop in Mississippi like I'd planned. Hell, that means I'm giving up a chance to get laid for this foolishness."

Mac grinned. "But what if Jesse James did hide some of his loot on your land? If I recall, he and his gang robbed a number of banks in and around the Missouri area."

Gavin frowned as he zipped up his gear and faced his friends. "There's not any loot on the Silver Spurs and nobody can convince me otherwise."

One

Layla Harris smiled as she accepted the plate of cookies. "Ms. Melody, I wished you wouldn't have gone to the trouble."

She said the words out of politeness, knowing they weren't true. Nobody could bake like Melody Blake and she was glad the older woman not only liked doing so but also enjoyed sharing her baked goods with Layla. Especially when the snack included a delicious tall glass of milk that had been produced right here on this ranch.

"No trouble at all," Melody Blake said, smiling. "Besides, I enjoy your company. It can get lonely in these parts."

Layla knew the Silver Spurs was a good half-hour car ride from town. At least Ms. Melody had neighbors living fairly close who checked in on her regularly. Layla had discovered the land owned by the majority of the people in this area had been in their families for generations and most of it was used for ranching cattle.

There was something special about the eighteen hundred acres encompassing the Silver Spurs and the spacious Blake family ranch home. Layla had felt welcomed the moment she had driven into the yard. The sprawling ranch house was massive and Layla figured it had to be over fifty-five hundred square feet. What she liked most was the wraparound porch with a swing that faced a beautiful pond.

Ms. Melody, a retired librarian, had said she didn't mind living in the huge house alone because she was used to it, and reading and baking kept her busy. The kitchen alone was massive and it was where the older woman spent a lot of her days, creating mouthwatering treats. In addition to the huge main house, there was a spacious guest cottage located within walking distance.

When Ms. Melody had agreed to let Layla conduct her archaeological dig on the property, she'd also kindly invited Layla to stay in the main house, but Layla preferred the guesthouse. She could come and go without disturbing the older woman.

According to Ms. Melody, the Silver Spurs had been a prosperous cattle ranch for years. It had even survived when the majority of the men, including Ms. Melody's husband, left to fight in the Vietnam War. When her husband and son became full-time military men, they'd hired a foreman to keep things running smoothly. Ms. Melody also explained that although her grandson was active in the military as a navy SEAL, whenever he returned home he reclaimed his role as a rancher.

Layla met Caldwell Andrews, the ranch foreman, and found the man pleasant and capable. The same held true for the men who worked for him. They appeared to be hard workers who were dedicated and loyal to the Blake family.

There was so much about Melody Blake that reminded Layla of her own grandmother. Both were independent, in the best of health for women their ages and were active in their churches and communities. Only thing, Gramma Candace wasn't a baker. She preferred spending her time with a knitting needle instead of a baking pan.

"I thought I'd bake chocolate chip cookies this time. They're Gavin's favorite," Ms. Melody said, breaking into Layla's musings.

At the mention of Ms. Melody's grandson, Layla couldn't dismiss the shiver that went through her body. Gavin Blake was a hunk. Although she'd never met him in person, she had seen enough of the man to judge his looks thanks to the numerous framed photographs that hung on several walls in this house. Layla knew it wasn't the man's ego that was responsible, but the grandmother who loved her grandson and was proud of the fact that, like the father and grandfather before him, he was a navy SEAL.

From all the photographs she'd seen, Layla could tell just how well built Gavin Blake was, how drop-dead gorgeous. He was definitely eye candy of the most delectable kind. Any woman would be hard-pressed not to feel some kind of sensual pull whenever she feasted her gaze on his image.

Layla had studied one of the close-up photos, which showed dimples when he smiled, a blunt nose, stubborn jaw and full lips. His angular face made him look so much like the warrior she'd heard him to be. She'd also heard he was quite the ladies' man. That bit of information had been shared by some of the locals she'd met at the café where she occasionally ate lunch. Once they'd heard she was about to dig on Blake property, they didn't hesitate to give her an earful.

According to a very talkative waitress whose eyes lit up whenever she spoke of Gavin, Layla had learned he had been a local football hero who had put Cornerstone, Missouri, on the map after leading his high school team to the state championship. No one had been surprised when he'd gone to the naval academy since he'd come from a military family. His father had been killed in the Gulf War and very little was known about his mother. Rumor had it that she'd been pretty, a few years younger than her husband and the two had married within a week of meeting in New York. Apparently, she'd never adjusted to being a military wife or living out on a ranch and had packed up and left. To this day she had never returned.

"Your grandson and I have something in common," Layla said, returning her thoughts to the conversation, "since chocolate chip cookies are my favorite, as well."

As she bit into a cookie, she thought that chocolate chip being their favorite was *all* she and Gavin had in common. Unlike him, she hadn't spent much time enjoying the opposite sex. She'd spent most of her life in school, getting her advanced degrees and working toward tenure with little time for male companionship. She had doctorates in History and Archaeology, and at twenty-six she was the youngest professor at Flintwood University in Seattle. That position had come with sacrifices such as limiting her social life, especially when it came to dating. The only people bothered by her decisions were her parents. They were hoping a man would come along and put a ring on her finger and a baby in her belly. She was their only child and they didn't hide the fact they wanted grandchildren.

Nor had they ever hidden the fact they weren't happy with her career choice. They were both gifted neurosurgeons and they'd expected her to follow in their footsteps by entering the medical field. They hadn't been pleased when she'd chosen not to do so. The thought of someone digging a hole in the ground instead of saving lives didn't make sense to them. But she'd never felt the calling to be a doctor, and she knew history was important, too. Understanding the past kept people from repeating their mistakes.

"So, Layla, what's the game plan for today?"

Layla smiled. She liked Ms. Melody's attitude. When Layla had shown up on the Blakes' doorstep over a week ago she hadn't known what to expect. She definitely hadn't been prepared for the older woman to believe her story about hidden treasure. She'd faced so much cynicism from colleagues regarding her research she'd come prepared to argue her points. Ms. Melody had listened and asked intelligent questions. Plenty of them. The older woman had also taken two days to review Layla's research, which had resulted in more questions. It was only then that Ms. Melody had agreed, with a request for periodic updates.

Ms. Melody had told Layla that her grandson would most likely not support her decision, but she'd also promised she would deal with him when the time came. Besides, she didn't expect him to return home for a few months, and it was highly likely the treasure would be found by then.

Layla hoped that was true. Her creditability with the university was on the line. The possibility of tenure was riding on the success of this dig and publication of her findings and techniques.

She'd participated in several excavations, but this would be the first one she'd spearheaded. Funds from the university hadn't been as much as she'd requested, due to budget cuts, but she was determined to make good use of what she'd been given and show results. The head of her department, Dr. Clayburn, hadn't offered much support. He'd even tried shifting the funds to another project. Lucky for her, he'd been out of the country when the vote had been taken.

She'd worked all her life for this chance to prove she was an archaeologist of note. If her research was correct—and she knew it was—she'd be the first one to find any of Jesse James's treasure, and she'd be the first to use some of the latest technology on a successful dig.

"Since all the permits are in order, I contacted the members of my team," she said, smiling. "They will be arriving in a week." Her excavation team consisted of students from the university, some from her classes and some from Dr.

Clayburn's. She had spoken with every one, and they were as anxious as she was to get started.

"You have to be excited about that."

"Yes," she answered, though she knew that's when the pressure would begin. "The equipment will start arriving on Monday." Layla took another bite into her cookie before adding, "Again, I really appreciate you letting us dig on your property, Ms. Melody." It showed Layla that Ms. Melody believed in her work.

"There's no need to thank me. Anyone who took the time to read your research with an open mind would reach the same conclusion. It's historically documented that James and his gang robbed a bank in Tinsel and then headed to east Missouri before a sheriff posse drove them south. I think you're right. Given how fast a horse can travel loaded down with a cache of gold bars, it makes perfect sense that the gang holed up somewhere in this area before taking a chance to continue east. And it makes even more sense that they got rid of some of their loot before heading toward the state line. Like I said, your research was thorough."

An inner glow filled Layla. Although others

had read the same documentation they couldn't forget her age or inexperience. Because of that, they assumed Layla was on a wild-goose chase, wasting university funds that were needed to finance more important archaeological projects.

At that moment they heard the sound of a vehicle pulling up in the yard.

Ms. Melody glanced over at the clock on the wall. "It's not even noon yet. I wonder who that could be."

Getting up from the table, Ms. Melody went over to the window and glanced out. When she turned back around, a huge smile covered her entire face. Layla heard the love in the older woman's voice when she said, "It's Gavin. He's home. The rancher returns."

Gavin grabbed his duffel bag from the truck before closing the door. He tilted his Stetson back on his head and looked at the car parked in front of what his grandmother called the guest cottage and what he called the party house. It was where he and his teammates would hang out whenever they visited.

Gavin hoped that his grandmother hadn't extended an invitation for the woman to stay on their property as well as dig on their land. If that was the case, he intended to send her packing quickly. He didn't want anyone taking advantage of his family.

He thought about what he was missing in Mississippi. He'd looked forward to being in bed with that bartender about now. Calling to cancel had been hard. Promising to head her way as soon as he'd taken care of this unexpected family emergency had satisfied her somewhat.

Walking around his truck, he took a deep breath of the Missouri air. This was home and he'd always enjoyed returning after every covert operation. Silver Spurs meant a lot to him. To his family. It was his legacy. It was land that had been in his family for generations. Land that he loved. He enjoyed being a rancher almost as much as he enjoyed being a SEAL. *Almost.* He would admit that being a SEAL was his passion.

Gavin appreciated having a good man like Caldwell to keep things running in his absence. The older man had done the same thing during Gavin's father's time. And Caldwell's father had been foreman to Gavin's grandfather, so Caldwell and his family also had deep history with the ranch.

While he was home, Gavin intended to return to ranching. He couldn't wait to get back in the saddle and ride Acer as well as help Caldwell and the men with the herd. And he needed to go over the books with Phil Vinson, the ranch's accountant.

However, the first thing on his agenda was a discussion with his grandmother about her giving someone permission to dig on their land. Hopefully he'd have everything settled by next week and he would hightail it to Mississippi. All he needed was one night with a woman and then he'd be good for a while.

He had taken one step onto the porch when the front door swung open and his grandmother walked out. She was smiling, and when she opened her arms, he dropped his duffel bag and walked straight into the hug awaiting him. She was petite, but her grip was almost stronger than that of a man. He loved and admired her so damn much. This was the woman who'd been there for him when his own mother had left. The woman who'd been there for him when he'd laid his father to rest sixteen years ago. She had, and always would be, his rock. That's why he refused to tolerate anyone trying to take advantage of her kindness.

"Welcome home, Gavin," she said, finally releasing him so she could lean back and look at him from head to toe as she always did when he returned from one of his assignments. "I didn't expect you for a few months yet. Did everything go okay?"

He smiled. She always asked him that knowing full well that because of the classified nature of his job, he couldn't tell her anything. "Yes, Gramma Mel, everything went okay. I'm back because I understand you and I need to—"

He glanced over his grandmother's shoulder and he blinked, not sure he was seeing straight. A woman stood in the doorway, but she wasn't just *some* woman. She had to be the most gorgeous woman he'd ever seen. Hell, she looked like everything he'd fantasized a woman to be, even while fully clothed in jeans and a pullover sweater. He didn't want to consider what his reaction would be if she was naked.

His grandmother sensed his attention had

shifted. She turned around and smiled at the woman. "Layla, come out here. I want you to meet my grandson."

Layla? Where had she come from? Was she the granddaughter of one of his grandmother's fellow church members or something? He recalled Mrs. Cotton had a granddaughter who visited on occasion from Florida and her name was Layla… or was it Liza? Hell, he couldn't remember. He wasn't thinking straight. When this Layla began walking toward him, he ceased thinking at all. She was wearing stretch jeans and a long sweater and had an eye-catching figure with curves in all the right places.

Gavin fought for air as she neared. He studied her features, trying to figure out what about them had him spellbound. Was it the caramel-colored skin, dark chocolate eyes, dimpled cheeks, button nose or well-defined kissable lips? Maybe every single thing.

Wow! Was he that hard up for a woman or did this Layla actually look *that* good? When she stopped beside him, a smile on her lips, he knew she actually looked that good. He kept his gaze trained on her face—even when he really wanted his eyes to roam all over her.

Not waiting for his grandmother to make introductions, his mouth eased into a smile. He reached out his hand and said, "Hello, I'm Gavin."

The moment their hands touched, a jolt of desire shot through his body. It's a wonder he hadn't lost his balance. Nothing like this had ever happened to him before and he touched women all the time. From the expression that had flashed in her eyes, he knew she had felt it, as well. Yes, there was definitely strong sexual chemistry between them.

"It's nice meeting you, Gavin," she said softly. He even liked the sound of her voice. "And I'm Layla. Layla Harris."

Harris? His horny senses suddenly screeched to a stop. Did she say Harris? Was Layla related to this Professor Harris? The woman's daughter perhaps? Was she part of the excavation team? She looked young, around twenty or twenty-one. Now he had even more questions and he was determined to get some answers when he had that little talk with his grandmother. "It's nice meeting you, too, Layla."

It was only when she eased her hand from his that he realized he still held it. She turned to his grandmother. "Thanks for the cookies and milk, Ms. Melody. I enjoyed them. I need to run into town to pick up a few items. Anything I can get for you while I'm there?"

"No. I've got everything I need."

Layla nodded. "Okay. I should be back in a couple of hours."

"Take your time."

Giving Gavin one last smile, she quickly walked down the steps toward the parked car. He stood and watched her every move until she was inside the car with the door closed. It was then that he turned his attention back to his grandmother. Not surprisingly, she was staring at him.

"For a minute I thought you'd forgotten I was standing here, Gavin Timothy Blake III," his grandmother said in an amused tone.

So he'd been caught ogling a woman. It hadn't been the first time and he doubted it would be the last. "What can I say, Gramma Mel?" He grinned sheepishly. "She's awfully pretty."

He decided not to mention how he appreciated

that sway to her hips when she walked, or how nice her breasts looked beneath her sweater.

"Yes, she is pretty. Come inside. Just so happens I baked some chocolate chip cookies this morning."

That made Gavin smile even wider as he picked up his duffel bag. His mouth watered just thinking about the cookies. Now if he could only get that image of Layla Harris's backside out of his mind...

"How are the rest of your teammates?" his grandmother asked, leading him through the front door. "You guys were together for over two months on this mission."

He glanced around as he entered. Everything looked the same. However, instead of smelling like vanilla, his grandmother's favorite scent, the house smelled of woman. Namely Layla Harris.

"Everyone is fine, just anxious to get home. Bane and his wife are renewing their vows in a few weeks and I plan to attend the ceremony," he said, placing his duffel bag on the sofa for now. "This was Coop's first covert operation after being rescued and he's good as ever."

The only reason Gavin shared that much info

with his grandmother was because when he'd come home last year before the holidays everyone had believed Coop had been killed on assignment. The entire team had taken Coop's death hard. Then right before Christmas, they'd found Coop was alive and being held hostage in the Syrian mountains. Gavin and his team had been sent in to get Coop, as well as other hostages, out alive.

"This was Bane's first time back, too, right?" his grandmother asked.

Did his grandmother not forget anything? Bane, being master sniper, had been recruited to work in DC for six months teaching SEAL recruits. "Yes, we were glad to have him back as well. And before I forget, I plan to head for Mississippi next week. I've got important business to take care of there." His grandmother didn't need to know that the important business was getting laid.

As soon as he entered the kitchen, he went straight to the sink to wash his hands and then quickly headed for the coffeepot. After pouring a cup, he turned and watched Gramma Mel arrange a half-dozen cookies on a plate for him.

He smiled. Anyone else would eat just one or two, but his grandmother knew him well. He needed at least a half dozen to get things started. "You need a fresh cup of coffee?" he asked her.

"Thanks. That would be nice, Gavin."

After pouring another cup, he moved away from the counter to sit down and she sat across from him. He placed her coffee in front of her and grabbed for a cookie. She slapped away his hand. "Say grace first."

He chuckled, recalling the protocol she expected of him. After quickly bowing his head in silence, he grabbed a cookie and almost swallowed it whole. He loved his grandmother's chocolate chip cookies.

She shook her head as she took a sip of her coffee. Now was as good a time as any to bring up what had brought him rushing back to the Silver Spurs. "What's this I hear about you giving some professor permission to dig on our land?"

Gramma Mel raised a brow over her cup of coffee. "And you know this how?"

He held his grandmother's gaze. "Sherman Lott called. He thought I had a right to know."

She frowned. "As far as I'm concerned, Sherman needs to mind his own business."

Gavin stared at this grandmother as he bit into another cookie. "The way I figure it, Caldwell is the one who should have called me. He's paid to keep me informed about what's going on around here. But he wouldn't call because he'd think doing so would be disloyal to you. And we both know what you mean to him."

His grandmother didn't say anything. She just stared into her cup of coffee. There really wasn't anything to say. Gavin had known for years that his grandmother and Caldwell had a thing going on. He wasn't stupid. Nor was he insensitive. He wanted the two people who meant the most to him to be happy. He figured that one day they would stop trying to be so damn discreet. In the meantime, what they did was their business. He'd only brought it up now to make a point.

"Caldwell would have told you had he thought it was important," his grandmother finally said.

"Whatever." He took a sip of his coffee. "So what about it? Did you give permission for a dig to take place on our property?"

She leaned back in her chair. "Yes, I gave my permission and I see nothing wrong with it."

Gavin kept his cool. "Well, I do. Honestly, Gramma Mel. You actually bought into this professor's tale about Jesse James's buried treasure?"

"Yes, I read her research and found it thorough and convincing. I have a copy, if you want to read it for yourself."

"I don't need to read anything to know the research is false. There's no buried treasure on our land, and I'm against the idea of anyone digging around for nothing."

His grandmother leaned forward in her chair. "And I happen to disagree. But what you believe is a moot point since I've given Layla permission and from what she told me this morning, her equipment will arrive in a few days—"

"Hold up," he said, giving the time-out sign with his hands. "Why did you give Layla Harris permission? It's her mother who's running things, right?"

His grandmother look confused. "Her mother? I never met the woman. Layla is in charge or should I say Dr. Layla Harris is in charge."

Surprise made Gavin raise his eyebrows. "Layla is the professor?"

"Yes, and a very competent one."

Gavin shook his head, not believing such a thing was possible. "She's young."

"She's twenty-six. However, I admit she does look younger."

Twenty-six? That was still young and yes, she definitely looked younger. He drew in a deep breath, trying to force back the memories of just how she'd looked…in her jeans and sweater. And then the thought that she'd deliberately oozed her way onto his grandmother's good side made him mad.

"You might have given your permission, but I have not given mine. Something that major means we need to be in full agreement."

"No, it doesn't. If you recall, we agreed that any time you were away on military business, I could make decisions in the best interest of the Silver Spurs."

"I don't consider digging up our land to be in the best interest of anything."

"I disagree. I'm excited about what Layla might

find. And I also gave her permission to stay in the guesthouse."

The line of Gavin's jaw tightened. He'd figured as much. Melody Blake was stubborn, but then so was he. He ate the last of his cookies, drained his coffee and stood. "I'm tired and need a full day of sleep. But we will talk about this again, Gramma Mel. In the meantime, I suggest you tell Dr. Layla Harris to hold up on bringing any type of equipment to the Silver Spurs."

And without saying anything else Gavin walked out of the kitchen.

Two

Layla pulled her car off on the shoulder of the road, unable to drive any farther. Once she killed her vehicle's ignition, she forced herself to breathe deeply a few times. Never in all her twenty-six years had any man wreaked havoc on her senses like Gavin Blake. Never had any man left her in such a mind-blowing sensuous state. Who would have thought a man could have her nerves dancing, her mind racing, her stomach swirling and her nipples actually feeling like they'd been stroked? She had been tempted to glide her hands over every inch of his sexy, sculpted body.

She had known he was the epitome of male perfection from all those photographs she'd seen. To be honest, that's where her troubles had started... with those photographs. In one, his lips had curved a little at the corners as he stared at her as if to say he knew exactly what she was thinking. She knew it was her wild imagination, but every time she glanced at that particular photo it was as if he was checking her out with those intense dark eyes of his. As if he knew her fantasies included him. Even in his photo, his muscular power had nearly overtaken her senses.

Pretty much like he'd done today. She hadn't counted on the real thing being even more explosive than his pictures. Before he'd realized she was in his grandmother's doorway, she had stood there spellbound as a rush of emotion made her body ache with desire. Then, when he'd noticed her, those eyes had made her yearn for something she didn't need. Something she had never needed. A man.

Gavin Blake had stood on his grandmother's porch wearing a pair of faded jeans and a T-shirt with his military tag hanging around his neck. Even wearing her sweater, she found the air cool, but the temperature hadn't seemed to faze him. Was he as hot-blooded as he looked?

The one thing she did know was that he was a big guy. Tall. Muscular. Built. She could imagine him as the football hero she'd heard he used to be, tackling players with little or no trouble. And she could definitely imagine him as a SEAL, taking on the bad guys to protect his country.

And she couldn't help but imagine him naked in bed…with her. Unfamiliar sensations raced through her just thinking about it. When he had touched her hand while staring into her eyes, she'd forgotten all about Ms. Melody standing there and had all but purred out loud. Blood had pounded through her entire body. She doubted she would ever use her hand again without remembering the feel of him. If her body reacted from a single touch to her hand, she didn't want to imagine him touching her anywhere else… her breasts, her stomach, between her legs. And when he smiled at her, she'd been a goner. She could still feel the impact in the pit of her stomach.

She had never experienced this kind of need in her life. She didn't even have a battery-operated boyfriend like some of her single female colleagues joked about owning. Sex was something that had never been on her must-do list. She'd put her energy into her academic career. But there was something about Gavin that made her think of heat and desire. Something that made the area at the juncture of her thighs quiver. Made her hormones sizzle.

Drawing in another deep breath, Layla admitted she needed to get a grip. She wasn't in Cornerstone, Missouri, to lust after the man who jointly owned the land she needed as an excavation site. All she wanted to do was stay on schedule and have a successful dig. Besides, Gavin Blake probably looked at other women the same way he'd looked at her. Hadn't that waitress in town enlightened Layla as to just what a ladies' man he was? Now seeing was believing.

Seeing was also a warning to keep her common sense intact and be on guard. An involvement with Gavin Blake was the last thing she needed, even though her body was trying to convince her otherwise.

There was something else she should be concerned about, something she just remembered.

Ms. Melody had said that her grandson might be against the idea of a dig on the Silver Spurs. Although Ms. Melody had given the okay, would Gavin's return change anything? The thought of losing the permission she'd gained sent nervous jitters through her.

Maybe she should talk to Gavin Blake herself. She would present her research to him the same way she'd presented it to Ms. Melody. Layla wanted to believe he was reasonable. It wasn't as if she would be digging all over his property. She had narrowed it to one location.

Yes, she would talk to him herself, but only after she talked to Ms. Melody—and after Layla convinced herself she could talk to him without every part of her turning to mush.

Gavin's eyes flew open and his entire body went on full alert. His ears picked up the sounds around him and it was then he recalled he was back in the United States and not in some godforsaken country where he had to be on guard 24/7.

It was always this way for the first few days after he returned home. He had to regroup and get his mind back in sync with normal life, deprogram from battle mode and ease back into the life of a rancher.

Glancing at the clock on his bedroom wall, he saw it was ten at night. He wasn't surprised that he'd slept nearly nine hours straight. His ears perked up at the sound that had woken him. Was that a harmonica? Granted it was far off, but he could still hear it. His teammates teased him about having sonic ears, because of his ability to hear a sound over a hundred feet away.

He wasn't sure if that was a blessing or a curse when he involuntarily eavesdropped on conversations he wished he hadn't. Like the time Mac was outside the barracks and downstairs in the yard talking to his wife on the phone, telling her in explicit sexual terms what he planned to do to her when he returned home from their mission. Gavin had heard every single word and the details had nearly burned his ears. They had definitely made him horny as hell. For a fleeting moment it had made him wish he had a wife or an exclusive woman he could return home to instead of a little black book filled with names of willing women.

Gavin pushed the whimsical thought from his

mind as he lay in bed and listened to the music. It sounded pretty damn good. He sat up and rubbed his hands across his face as if to wipe away the sleep. Pushing the bedcovers aside, he eased out of bed. Not bothering to cover his naked body, he strolled over to the window, pushed aside the curtain and looked out. The October air produced a chill that would send shivers through a normal person's body. But because of his SEAL training, Gavin could withstand temperatures of the highest and lowest extremes.

The way the moonlight crested the rocky bluffs, dissecting the valleys and rolling plains, was simply breathtaking. There was nothing more beautiful than Silver Spurs at night. For as long as he could remember, he'd always been moved by the grandeur of the land he was born on.

The harmonica stopped and he knew the sound had come from the party house where Layla was staying. Since the woman was still in residence, he could only assume his grandmother had not delivered his message. Had she done so he was certain Professor Layla Harris would have left by now.

Maybe he should talk to Layla Harris himself.

Make it clear where he stood. He moved back toward the bed. Instead of getting into it, Gavin ignored the voice of reason saying he should wait and talk to Layla in the morning and grabbed his clothes off the chair. After sliding into his jeans he tugged his T-shirt over his head. He put on his socks and boots and headed for the door.

The music from the harmonica started up again.

Layla placed her harmonica aside. Playing it relaxed her and she would always appreciate her grandfather for teaching her. She could vividly recall those summers when she would sit on the front porch of her grandparents' New Orleans home and listen to her grandfather play his harmonica, then beg him to teach her how. When Grampa Chip passed away ten years ago, his request had been that she play the harmonica at his funeral and she had.

Thoughts of losing the grandfather she adored always made her sad and that was the last emotion she wanted to feel right now. Even when she had no idea what would happen with this dig, she wanted happy thoughts. Earlier, Ms. Melody assured Layla that all was well. Her grandson was too exhausted to think straight and he needed a full day of sleep.

Layla hoped that was good news considering she had all that machinery on the way. She figured Ms. Melody knew her grandson better than Layla did. She would wait for Gavin Blake to get his full day of sleep. Hopefully, after another discussion with Ms. Melody, he would see things the way his grandmother did.

Layla glanced around the guest cottage, thinking how much she liked it here. The place was larger than her apartment in Seattle. She definitely didn't have a huge living room with a fireplace or a spacious master bedroom with a large en suite bath with a walk-in shower and Jacuzzi tub. The cottage also had a loft that could be used as additional sleeping space, and an eat-in kitchen. She loved the wood floors throughout and the high ceilings. And because it sat a distance away from the main house, she could play her harmonica without worrying about disturbing anyone. That was something she couldn't do at her own apartment.

She stood to stretch and was about to head toward the bedroom when she heard a knock on the door. Glancing at the clock on the wall she saw it was after ten. Usually Ms. Melody was in bed every night by eight since she was such an early riser. Had something happened? Had the older woman decided not to butt heads with her grandson and didn't want Layla and her team to dig on the Silver Spurs after all?

Layla moved toward the door. It didn't have a peephole so she leaned against the wooden frame and asked, "Who is it?"

"Gavin. Gavin Blake."

Her gaze widened and heat swirled around in her lower belly. She tried forcing the sensations aside. Why would Gavin seek her out at this time of night? Had something happened to Ms. Melody? From their talks, she knew the older woman suffered occasionally with migraines.

She opened the door and the man stood there, almost bigger than life, and looking as yummy as a chocolate sundae. He was dressed as he had been that morning. Jeans. T-shirt. Western boots. But her brain wasn't computing *what* he was wearing as much as *how well* he was wearing it.

Although it was cold, he wasn't even wearing a jacket. He leaned in the doorway looking exactly like any woman's dream. Hot. Sexy. And then some. He was one of those can't-get-to-sleep nighttime fantasies that left you hot and bothered with no relief in sight. It was those thoughts that had her unable to speak, so she just stood there and stared at the penetrating dark gaze holding hers as her heart beat violently in her chest.

She knew SEALs stayed in shape, but the body of the man standing before her was simply ridiculous. She knew of no other man whose body was so well built. So magnificently toned. His jeans appeared plastered to him in the most decadent way. He made her think of wicked temptation and sinful delights.

Doubting she could stand there much longer without going up in flames, even with the blast of cold air, she swallowed deeply and then forced her voice to ask, "Is something wrong with Ms. Melody?"

From the look that quickly flashed across his features, she could tell he was surprised by her question. "What makes you think something is wrong with my grandmother?"

Layla sighed deeply. "What other reason would bring you here?"

That, Gavin thought, was a good question. Why *was* he here? He had heard the harmonica. And had quickly figured out the source was Layla in the party house. So what had driven him out into the night? He definitely could have waited until morning to talk to her about the dig. Had he come here just to stand in the doorway to try and get his fill of looking at her?

"Gavin?"

And why did the sound of his name from her lips send desire throbbing through him? In his horny state, it wouldn't take much to push him over the edge. "Yes?"

"If nothing is wrong with Ms. Melody, why are you here?"

He crossed his arms over his chest. "I heard you playing a harmonica."

Layla's jaw dropped in surprise. She must have been shocked that he heard her. The guest cottage was far away from the main house and on the opposite side of the bedrooms. Gramma Mel had probably told her he would be sleeping hard for a full day.

But he wasn't sleeping. He was here. He rubbed

his hand down his face in frustration. He needed to get to Mississippi fast or else...

Or else what? He would begin thinking of Layla Harris in his bed? Too late. His mind had already gone there. More than once. Those thoughts had pretty much settled in the moment he'd laid eyes on her. Having her at the party house wasn't helping matters. Typically, all he had to do was snap his fingers to get any woman he wanted. Why were his fingers itching to be snapped? With Layla Harris, would it be that easy? Why didn't he think so?

"I am so sorry," she said now. "I didn't mean to wake you. I know you need to get all that rest and—"

"You didn't wake me."

"But you said that you heard me playing."

"I did, but that's not what awakened me." Gavin figured there was no reason to tell her how disrupted his sleep patterns tended to be during his first few days back home. Which still left her question unanswered. Why was he here? Why had he sought her out? In the middle of the night? "You play very well," he said.

Gavin thought she was even more beautiful

than she had looked this morning. He blamed the easy smile that touched her lips.

"Thanks, but I'm sure you didn't come all this way just to give me that compliment."

No, he hadn't. He'd actually come to give her hell for feeding his grandmother a bunch of crock about buried treasure on their land. So he needed to say what he had come to say. "We should talk. May I come in?"

It was funny he would ask. After all, she was the visitor on his land. This was his house. Ms. Melody had told her that Gavin and some of his SEAL teammates had built it a few years ago as a place to hang out whenever they visited.

Gavin and his friends could get loud and rowdy here at the cottage without disturbing his grandmother. That accounted for why the place was so spacious with the cupboards bare—except for a refrigerator stocked with beer and wine coolers. Not to mention that a deck of cards seemed to be in every room.

"Yes, of course you can come in. You own the place."

"But you're my grandmother's guest."

Had he said that to remind her she wasn't *his* guest? To remind her that her presence on the Silver Spurs was something he didn't support? Layla would find out soon enough.

She moved from the door and he followed, closing it behind him. "Would you like something to drink?" Grinning brightly, she said, "There's plenty of beer and wine coolers in the fridge."

Gavin chuckled. "I'll take a beer."

She nodded. "One beer coming up." She felt his gaze on her backside.

"Here you are. I feel funny doing this," Layla said, coming back into the room carrying a cold bottle of beer.

He lifted a brow. "Doing what?"

"Serving you your own beer."

"No reason that you should. You're my grandmother's guest."

That was the second time he'd said that, Layla thought. Not one to beat around the bush, she crossed the room to hand him the beer, and then wished she hadn't. Their hands had only briefly touched so why was heat filling her? And why was he looking at her as if that same heat filled him?

She quickly took a step back and wiped her hands down the sides of her jeans.

"You think that will get rid of it?"

She met his eyes. She knew what he'd insinuated, but she wanted to be sure. "Get rid of what?"

"Nothing."

He then opened the bottle and took a huge gulp. Afterward, he licked his lips while she watched. Her chest tightened. He lowered the bottle from his mouth and held her gaze. "Want a sip?"

She drew in a deep breath to clamp down on her emotions. Was he offering to share his beer? For them to drink from the same bottle? Doing something like that was way too intimate for her. Evidently not for him. A distinct warmth coiled around her midsection. The way his eyes darkened wasn't helping matters.

She should call his bluff and take a sip. But that might lead to other things. It might give him ideas. The same ideas floating crazily through her head. The last thing she needed was an involvement with a man. Any man. Especially him. Her work was too important to her. The idea of an October fling was not. "No thanks. I had one earlier and one was enough for me."

Instead of saying anything, he nodded and raised the bottle to his lips to drain the rest. She watched his throat work. When had seeing a man drink anything been a turn-on?

When he finished the bottle and lowered it, she asked, "Want another one?"

He smiled at her. "No, one was enough for me."

She couldn't help but smile back at his use of her words. "I don't know, Gavin Blake. You seem like the sort of guy that could handle a couple of those."

"You're right, but that's not why I'm here."

His words were a reminder that he hadn't shown up tonight for chitchat and drinking beer. "Yes, you said you wanted to talk. Is there a problem?" Layla knew there was and figured he was about to spell it out for her.

"Who taught you to play the harmonica?"

She'd expected him to just dive in. His question threw her. "My grandfather," she said, angling her head to look up at him. "He was the best. At least most people thought so."

"And who was your grandfather?"

"Chip Harris."

Surprise made Gavin's jaw drop. "Chip Harris? *The* Chip Harris?"

Layla nodded. "Yes," she said, intentionally keeping her voice light. Very few people knew that. It wasn't something she boasted about, although she was proud of her grandfather's success and accomplishments. He'd been a good man, a great humanitarian and a gifted musician. But most of all he had been a wonderful grandfather. Her grandparents had helped to keep her world sane during the times her parents had made it insane.

Layla saw Gavin's dark, penetrating eyes suddenly go cold. "Is anything wrong?"

"So that's how you did it."

She raised a brow. "That's how I did what?"

"How you were able to talk my grandmother into going along with your crazy scheme of Jesse James's treasure being buried on my property. You probably heard she's a big fan of Chip Harris, and used the fact that you're his granddaughter to get in good with her. Get Gramma Mel to trust you and—"

"You jerk." Anger flared through her. His accusations filled her with rage. "How dare you accuse me of doing something so underhanded, so unethical and low? You might not know me but you know your grandmother. How can you think so little of her to imagine she has such a weak mind she could be taken in by anyone? How can you not trust her judgment?"

Layla drew in a disgusted breath and then added furiously, "For your information, I never once mentioned anything about my relationship to Chip Harris to her. Ms. Melody's decision was based on my research, which she took the time to read. And she asked questions and found some of her own answers. So regardless of what you believe, her decision was based on facts, Gavin Blake. Facts and nothing more."

Gavin was stunned by Layla's rage. When her words sank in, he regretted accusing her of manipulating Gramma Mel. He'd crossed the line and he knew it. He owed her an apology. "I'm sorry. I should not have accused you of that."

"But you did. Save your apology for your grandmother. She's one of the most intelligent women I know. But tonight you made her out to be a woman who can be influenced easily by anything, especially name-dropping. Like I said, you should know your grandmother better than that."

Gavin didn't say anything. Probably because he knew she was right. His grandmother was as sharp as a tack. She'd told Layla so many stories of how he'd tried to pull one over on her... unsuccessfully. Maybe he should do what his grandmother had done and read Layla's report for himself.

"I should not have come here tonight," he finally said.

"No, you should not have, especially if you came to talk that kind of BS. I don't have time for it."

Layla's words seemed to irritate him. "You don't think I have a right to question why you're here?"

She didn't back down. In fact she took a step closer. "You have every right. But you already know why I'm here. If you don't agree with your grandmother or you want to question why I feel a dig on the Silver Spurs is warranted, I can understand that. But what you did, Gavin, is question my integrity. I take that personally."

"You have to admit the idea of buried treasure on my land is pretty far-fetched."

"Maybe to you but not to me. You're a SEAL. I'm sure there are times when you engage in covert operations where the facts lead you to believe your assignment will be successful…although logically it doesn't seem possible."

He frowned. "It's not the same."

"I think it is. I did my research on the life of Jesse James. Five years' worth. I studied his life, specifically that bank robbery in Tinsel. That's what led me here. If you took the time to read my research, you would see it's all there. All I'm asking is for you to give me the same courtesy Ms. Melody did and take the time to read my work."

"I don't have to read a report to know what you're claiming isn't true."

In frustration, Layla blew out a breath and threw up her hands. "Why are you so stubborn?"

Instead of answering he gave her a careless shrug of his broad shoulders. "I'm not being stubborn. Just realistic."

He wasn't even trying to be reasonable. "So what do you want, Gavin? Since you believe that I've hoodwinked your grandmother and I'm a lunatic on the hunt for buried treasure, did you come here tonight to ask me to leave? To tell me to get off your property because you won't allow me and my team to dig?"

When he didn't say anything but continued to stare down at her with those dark, penetrating eyes of his, she knew what she'd just said was true. "Fine. I'll leave in the morning."

She moved with the intention of walking around him to show him the door. He surprised her when he reached out and grabbed her arm. The moment he touched her it seemed every hormone in her body sizzled. She couldn't move away from him. His hand skimmed down her arm in a sensual caress.

"What do you think you're doing?" She heard the tension in her voice and felt her heart rate quicken. Their gazes held and something hot in the depths of his eyes held her hostage. She wanted to break eye contact and couldn't. How could any one man have so much sex appeal? Create such primal attraction?

Layla became angry with herself because of her reaction to him. The man standing in front of her had destroyed her plans. He'd placed her in a difficult position with the administration at the university and with her team. She'd have to cancel excavation and lose her funding. She might never get another chance to prove her theories. Yet at that moment all she could think about was how fully aware of him she was.

"What I'm doing is touching you," he answered moments later, as if he'd needed time to give her question some thought.

Well, she had news for him. He should keep his hands to himself. So why wasn't she telling him that? And why was there a throb inside her? One that had started in her stomach but was now going lower to the juncture of her thighs? And why, when she saw his head lowering, did she just stand there? When his lips touched hers and he wrapped her in his arms, she sank into him. The same way he was sinking into her mouth.

The kiss was making her forget everything, even the fact that he wanted to throw her off his ranch. The only thing she could concentrate on was how his tongue was moving around in her mouth, sending shivers up her spine until she heard herself moan.

But he was moaning as well, and then he deep-

ened the kiss. She recognized this for what it was.
Lust. And that usually led to sex. If that was his
plan, he could take it elsewhere. She had no intention of getting involved, no matter how fleet-
ingly, with a man who refused to take her work
seriously.

She pulled her mouth free and took a step back.
"Like I said. I'll be off your property in the morning." She then walked around him to the door.

Before opening it, she glanced back at him. He
stood in the same spot, staring at her as if she was
a puzzle he was trying to figure out. Seriously?
Did he think she was that complicated? As far as
she was concerned, he was the problematic one.

He was the man who, with very little effort, it
seemed, could tempt her to lower her guard, to
surrender to this need he created inside of her.
A need she hadn't realized even existed. And
it appeared he was dealing with his own need
if the huge bulge pressing against the zipper of
his jeans was anything to go by. There were just
some things an aroused man couldn't hide.

"We need to keep sex out of this, Gavin." She'd
had to say it, considering the strong sexual chem-

istry flowing between them. Chemistry both of them were fully aware of.

He stared at her for a long moment, saying nothing, but she saw the tightening of his jaw. Had her words hit a nerve? Had they made him realize that she wasn't as gullible as he thought?

When he began walking toward her, her heartbeat quickened with every step he took. Never had she felt such a strong primal attraction to any man. Even his walk, his muscled thighs flexing erotically with every step, tripped her pulse. It had her drowning in the sexual vibes pouring off him.

When he came to a stop in front of her, he grabbed her hand to keep her from opening the door. Immediately, like before, they became attuned to each other. Why was there such a strong physical attraction between them? No man had ever made her forget about work. But she struggled to remember that work was the reason she was here. That and nothing else.

"Don't know about you, but I can't keep sex out of it, Layla. I think you know why. Whether we like it or not, there's a strong sensual pull between us. I felt it the moment I set eyes on you this morning, and if you say you didn't feel it as well, then you would be lying. You might pretend otherwise, but you want me as much as I want you."

No matter what he said, she would deny it. She hadn't come to the ranch for this. She had come to Cornerstone, Missouri, to do a job—to prove her theory and move up in her career—*not* to have an affair with a navy SEAL who could overtake her senses. A man who was proving, whether she wanted him to or not, that she had sexual needs she'd ignored for too long. But regardless of that proof, under no circumstances would she sleep with him. Doing so would be a very bad idea. It would be a mistake that could cost her all she'd worked for up to this point. Besides, hadn't he all but told her to get off his land?

Instead of a straight-out denial, she said, "What I want is to be allowed to do my job. I need to do that dig, Gavin."

His gaze hardened. "Why? To prove me wrong?"

"More than proving you wrong, I need to prove to myself and my peers that I am right. There's a difference, but I don't expect you to understand."

* * *

Yes, he understood the difference. Hadn't he felt the need to prove that he was his own man? To prove that being a SEAL hadn't been about his grandfather's and father's legacies but about establishing a legacy of his own? The first Gavin Blake had been handpicked to be part of the first special operations unit that became known as the SEALs. And Gavin's father, Gavin Blake Jr, had died a war hero after rescuing his team members and others who'd been held hostage during Desert Storm.

For years, he'd thought being Gavin Blake III was a curse more than a blessing. You couldn't share the name of bigger-than-life SEAL predecessors without some people believing you should be invincible. It had taken years to prove to others, as well as to himself, that he was his own man. Free to make his own mistakes. Now he cherished the memories of the heroes his grandfather and father had been and he was proud to carry their names and to continue the family legacy of being a SEAL. In the end, he'd realized becoming his own man hadn't been about proving anything to others but proving it to himself.

A part of him wanted to believe that Layla's issues were hers alone. They were her business to deal with and not his. But for some reason he couldn't let her go. His curiosity pushed him to say, "Don't leave the Silver Spurs just yet, Layla."

He saw that his words surprised her. Gave her pause. "Why? You ridiculed my years of research, accused me of manipulating your family and told me not to dig on your land. Why should I stay?"

"To convince me that you're right."

He could tell from her expression she thought what he'd said didn't make sense. "I can't do that unless you give me permission to excavate, Gavin. That's the only way I can prove anything."

Gavin was totally captivated by Layla Harris— by her passion for her work, and this passion between them. Why? He wasn't sure. She was beautiful, but he'd been around beautiful women before. She was built—with lush curves, a nice backside and very attractive features—but all those were just physical attributes. Deep down, he believed there was more to Layla Harris than just her beauty, more than her intelligence. There was something inside of her she refused to let surface. And it was something he wanted to uncover.

One thing for certain, he honestly wasn't ready for her to leave the Silver Spurs. But she was right. Why should she stay if he wouldn't allow her to dig on his property? He gritted his teeth at the thought of any woman making him feel so needy that he'd allow her to dig up the south pasture, his special place. But he quickly remembered he'd gone six months without sex, which had a way of crippling a man's senses.

"It's late," he heard himself say. "Let's talk more tomorrow."

"Will talking tomorrow change anything, Gavin?"

All he knew for certain was that he couldn't think straight being this close to her. But the last thing he wanted was to wake up tomorrow and find her gone. "It might," he said. "I'm not making any promises, Layla. All I can say is that right now I'm exhausted and can't think straight." He would let her think his muddled mind was due to exhaustion and not the degree of desire he had for her.

"Will you read my research?"

He wouldn't lie about that. "No. You can go over the important aspects of your work when we meet tomorrow."

She stared at him for a long moment as if weighing his words. Finally, she said, "Alright. I'll stay until we can talk."

Relief poured through his body, quickly followed by frustration and annoyance. No woman could tie him in knots like Layla seemed capable of doing. "I'll see you tomorrow."

When he'd first arrived, her hair had been neatly pulled back. Had he mussed up her hair when he'd kissed her? Maybe that was why the loose curls now teasing her forehead were a total turn-on.

"Good night, Gavin."

That was his cue to go. "Good night." He opened the door and stepped out into the cold Missouri night.

Three

Layla awakened the next morning wondering what she'd gotten herself into. Would remaining an additional day to meet with Gavin really change his mind?

There was always the possibility that it could, which was the reason her bags were not already packed. Besides, she was a fighter, a person who didn't give up easily. It had taken over a year to convince the university to give her funding for the dig, and another six months to get them to ease off some of their restrictions and ridiculous conditions. Even now, she wasn't sure the heads of the department believed in her 100 percent, but at least they were giving her a chance.

Now all of that forward momentum—the work that could change the history books and earn her a tenured position—could end because of Gavin. She drew in a deep breath. What was she going to do? Short of sleeping with him, she would do just about anything to convince him to reconsider.

She shifted in bed to look out the window. She'd thought she had a beautiful view in her high-rise apartment overlooking downtown Seattle—until now. The rolling plains, majestic hills and valleys of the Silver Spurs were awesome. The concrete jungle she saw each morning from her bedroom window couldn't compare.

She loved it here. She wouldn't mind returning to visit. But this time, she wasn't here for a vacation. She had a job to do and she hoped Gavin wouldn't stand in the way of her doing it.

Gavin.

He thought she'd been manipulative enough to use her musician grandfather's name to get in good with his grandmother. Although he had apologized, those accusations still bothered her. Yet in spite of them, she had allowed him to kiss her. And it was a kiss she couldn't stop thinking about. A kiss so deeply entrenched in her mind that she'd thought about it even while she'd slept. She was thinking about it now while wide-awake.

Layla realized that kissing, something she'd never enjoyed doing before, wasn't so bad after all. At least with Gavin it wasn't bad. Evidently other guys had lacked his expertise. Not only did he have a skillful tongue, but he knew how to use it. The feel of being in his strong arms had sent pleasure throughout her entire body.

She drew in a sharp breath as memories flooded her, filling her with a longing for them to kiss again. Yet how could she even contemplate repeating that kiss when she wasn't sure she even liked him? The one thing she did know was that she definitely desired him and he'd been arrogant enough to call her out on that.

In frustration, she rubbed a hand down her face. She needed to rid her mind of thoughts of Gavin. She'd never mixed business with pleasure and she had no intention of doing so now. The most important thing in her life had always been her work, and she deliberately avoided relationships to keep her focus where it should be. She wouldn't let her attraction to Gavin interfere with what she needed to do.

And the first thing she needed to do was get out of bed and start her day. Gavin said they would talk today and she could only hope for the best.

It was early evening when Gavin finally opened his eyes and he immediately thought about the woman staying in the party house. The woman he'd kissed last night.

Layla had mated her tongue to his with an intensity that made every muscle in his body throb. It was as if she had just as much passion bottled up inside as he did. And he'd unleashed it all with that kiss.

He would love to pick up where they'd left off last night. Take the passion to a whole new level. That made him think of other things…like making love to Layla. How it would feel to run his hands through her hair, lock his mouth and his body to hers. Become immersed in all that sexual energy they seemed to generate. He got hard just thinking about the possibilities.

Gavin glanced over at the clock. He had slept the day away, but he had needed the sleep. Images of Layla had sneaked into the deep recesses of his mind, whether he had wanted them to or not. She'd been in his dreams.

He wanted her.

There. He'd confirmed it in his mind without an ounce of regret. He was a man with needs and that kiss last night had totally obliterated any desire for the Mississippi vixen. He'd lost interest in heading south as planned. Nor did he want Layla to leave the ranch. But like she'd reminded him last night, unless he agreed to let her dig on the property, she had no reason to stay.

That meant he had to come up with a plan.

He rubbed sleep from his eyes, remembering that he had detected a few insecurities lurking within Layla last night. Something about her need to prove herself. What was that about? Did he really want to know? Did he even care?

Yes, he cared. He would go so far as to say that he even admired her spunk. Layla was tough and he had a feeling he hadn't even seen half the strength she possessed. She had to be resilient to have become a college professor at such a young age. He could see her holding her own when it mattered. He couldn't help but smile when he recalled her saying that he needed to keep sex out of this situation. Little did she know he had no intention of doing that. Their attraction was too strong and he intended to use it to his advantage.

As he stood to head for the bathroom, he halted upon hearing voices. They were his grandmother's and Layla's. His body immediately reacted to the sound of Layla's voice. They were in the kitchen. And he could tell his grandmother was enjoying the conversation.

He could understand why Gramma Mel was so taken with Layla. Although he never thought about it much, his grandmother probably got lonely around here whenever he was away. Even though she had Caldwell, there hadn't been another woman staying on the Silver Spurs since Gavin's mother had left.

He tried pushing thoughts of Jamie Blake from his mind like he'd always done. Why should he think about the woman who hadn't thought of him? One day she'd packed up and left, drove away leaving only a letter claiming she needed time away and would return. She never did. That's what had bothered Gavin the most, knowing a woman could just walk away from her husband and eight-year-old son without looking back.

Refusing to think about his mother anymore, Gavin entered his bathroom to shower. He hoped Layla stayed in the kitchen with his grandmother for a while because he definitely needed to talk to her.

Layla's hand tightened on her glass of iced tea the moment Gavin entered the kitchen. She didn't have to glance behind her to know he was there. His presence filled the room and sent all kinds of sensations vibrating through her. She was a little irritated that she was so aware of him. The sexual chemistry she'd hoped was a fluke was back in full force.

"Gavin, I figured the smell of food would wake you sooner or later," Melody Blake said, smiling at her grandson.

When he moved into Layla's line of vision she had no choice but to glance over at him. "Yes, it definitely did," he said, answering his grandmother but staring straight at Layla.

Then he spoke to her. "Layla. How are you today?"

She wanted to tell him she'd been fine until he'd made an appearance. She couldn't stop her gaze from roaming all over him. He stood near the window and the fading afternoon light highlighted his features, his clothing, everything about him. Not for the first time, Layla thought he had to be the sexiest man alive.

When he lifted a brow, she realized she had yet to answer his question. "I'm fine, Gavin. Thanks for asking."

She quickly switched her gaze away from him and back to her plate. Why had she waited so long to answer? Doing so had made it obvious she'd been checking him out. Thoroughly.

"I left your food warming in the oven, Gavin," Ms. Melody said, breaking the tension.

"Thanks, Gramma Mel. All I've been able to think about these last few days was getting back to your home-cooked meals." Gavin opened the oven to peek inside.

After getting his plate out of the oven, he smiled at Layla and crossed the kitchen to sit in the chair beside her, brushing his thigh against hers. He said grace and then lifted his head and looked over at Layla. He caught her staring at him again. She knew his touch had been no accident. Totally deliberate.

He pasted an innocent smile on his face and asked, "So, Layla, how was your day?"

Layla gritted her teeth. The nerve of him asking how her day had gone when she'd been waiting to meet with him. She hadn't mentioned anything about Gavin's visit last night to Ms. Melody. There was no way Layla could have mentioned it with a straight face, especially when she couldn't help thinking of the kiss they'd shared.

Knowing he was waiting for her response, she said, "My day has been going great."

"Gavin, I'm glad I got to say hello before I leave," his grandmother said, standing to her feet.

Gavin looked at his grandmother. "Where are you going?"

"The civic center. It's bingo night and Viola is picking me up. She should be here any minute."

It suddenly occurred to Layla that she would be left alone with Gavin. That shouldn't be a big deal since they still needed to talk, but it was. Already nerves stirred in the pit of her stomach.

"We'll take care of the kitchen," she heard Gavin say. "Layla and I need to talk anyway."

Ms. Melody looked back and forth at the two of

them before directing her gaze to her grandson. "I think that's a good idea." At the sound of the car horn, a smile touched her lips. "That's Viola."

Before Layla and Gavin could tell her good-bye, Melody Blake had grabbed her purse and was out the door.

That's when Gavin turned his attention back to Layla.

When Gavin saw Layla loading her dishes into the sink, he said, "You don't have to help me with the dishes."

She shrugged her shoulders. "I don't mind."

Her back was to him and he couldn't stop his gaze from covering every inch of her backside, wrapped tight in her skirt. And before she'd left the table, more than once he'd checked out her pink blouse, noticing the deep V neck. There was nothing like seeing a little of a woman's cleavage every now and then. Made him wonder what her breasts looked like. How they would feel in his hands. Taste in his mouth.

"Your grandmother forgot to mention she made a dessert," Layla said, breaking into his thoughts and turning around to meet his gaze.

"What is it?"

"Peach cobbler. Do you want some?"

That question was not one she should be asking him. Not when he had an erection nearly hard enough to burst out of his jeans. Yes, he wanted some, but his thoughts weren't on the peach cobbler.

Why did the picture of her standing at his grandmother's sink make a pang of desire shoot through him? The hair she'd worn down and around her shoulders yesterday was now confined in a ponytail. It wouldn't take much to walk across the room and set it free. After doing that, he would proceed to do all kinds of naughty things to her. Gavin shifted in his seat to relieve the pressure against his zipper.

"Yeah, I'd love to have some," he said in a deep, husky voice. And he knew Layla had figured out they weren't talking about peach cobbler.

She didn't say anything, just stared at him. He wished she didn't look so damn sexy while she sized him up, trying to figure him out. There wasn't much to find out on that score. He was a horny bastard and would remain so until he'd taken care of his sexual needs. That meant they needed to talk, and the sooner the better.

"We can talk while eating peach cobbler," he said.

Layla seemed relieved to finally begin their discussion and returned to the table with two plates of peach cobbler. "Where do we start?" she asked, sliding one of the plates in front of him before sitting down.

He picked up his fork and looked over at her. "We can start by talking about us."

Her expression clearly said that wasn't what she thought they should be talking about. "We agreed to discuss the dig and not this thing between us."

Gavin wondered if Layla knew that "this thing" actually had a name. It was called physical desire. "I think we should talk about us before discussing the dig."

She gave him an annoyed look. "Why? I told you last night we needed to keep sex out of it."

Yes, she had said that, but did she actually think they could keep sex out of it when there was so much chemistry between them? So much that even now he would have no problem taking her right here on this damn table? "You're an intelligent woman, Layla. I'm sure you're well aware of how the human body operates. All of us have needs."

"Speak for yourself, Gavin."

He watched her nervously gnaw on her lower lip and heated lust danced up his spine. He was trying like hell to figure her out. Was she denying she had needs, as well? He knew from last night's kiss that that was a lie. Her denial made Gavin wonder about her experience level.

"Are you saying you don't want to have sex with me?"

As if the question shot her to full awareness, she leaned over the table and glared at him. "I don't want to have sex with you, Gavin. I don't want to have sex with anybody. All I want is to do my job. A job you refuse to let me do."

They weren't getting anywhere. For some reason he didn't want to talk to her about the dig until he found out why she kept certain emotions in check. So he tried another approach.

"Tell me about yourself, Layla."

Layla lifted a brow. That was clearly not what she'd expected. "I graduated from high school at sixteen and immediately went to college. Graduated with my bachelor's degree in history, then went on to get a master's in archaeology. My doctorate is in both history and archaeology."

"And you're just twenty-six?"

"Yes. I went to college year-round. I've worked on dig sites as an undergrad and while working toward my PhD so this won't be my first excavation."

"But it will be the first one you've been in charge of, right?"

"Yes, that's true."

He leaned back in his chair, deciding to keep her talking about the dig for a while, after all. He doubted she realized that whenever she talked about her work she lowered her guard. "So you admit you're inexperienced."

Layla frowned. He could tell she wasn't sure if they were still talking about the dig. "I don't think of myself as inexperienced, Gavin, so you shouldn't think that, either."

"Then tell me what I should think."

After several moments, she said, "You should focus on the fact that my being here is the result of several years of research. I didn't just wake up one morning and decide to do this. I've tracked each and every one of James's bank robberies in this area. Mapped out every possible trail he could have taken, every single place he and the gang could have hidden out. Then I obtained records of this land and the surrounding properties. I had my team digitally re-create how this area would have looked back then.

"The Silver Spurs would have been the ideal place to stop over because of the low-hanging trees. And the lake between here and the Lotts' spread would have allowed the gang time to wash away their scent and stay hidden from the sheriff's posse. I could even see James's gang being smart enough to use a decoy to send the posse racing in another direction. One away from here to give them time to bury their loot and lighten their load."

Gavin was trying not to get caught up in the sound of her voice. He wanted to hear the words she was saying. She was excited about her work and discussing it energized her. He couldn't help noticing the glow in her eyes, the confidence in her voice, the smile on her lips. The same lips he had tasted last night.

She was trying like hell to convince him that

she was onto something, that she had researched her findings and believed in everything she was telling him. He knew there had to be a number of doubters...like himself.

When she stopped talking, he shifted his gaze from her lips to her eyes. "I take it you've already surveyed the area, used ground penetrating radar on the location already."

She nodded. If she was surprised by his knowledge of her preliminary assessment, she didn't show it. "I've gone further. I was able to get an infrared spectrum."

He lifted a brow. "How?"

"One of my students is big into digital technology and created it for me. That's the advantage I have over others working on this subject, I'm bringing this excavation into the digital age."

The technological aspect was an area Gavin was somewhat familiar with. The military already used all sorts of futuristic developments. It was important whenever they were sent into enemy territory that they didn't step on booby traps or buried explosives.

She looked at him expectantly, as if he would question what she said. He merely nodded. "I'm familiar with the use of high-tech digital to detect buried items."

She smiled, obviously glad that he was following her. "All the equipment my team and I use is state-of-the-art, some have never before been used in an archaeological context and they were developed exclusively for this dig by students in my department," she said proudly.

Because she was young he couldn't imagine her getting others to rally behind her for the cause. Whether she knew it or not, that spoke volumes about her character as a leader. It would take a strong individual to coax others on board. He knew how that could be.

"It's too late today but tomorrow I want to check out the area you've targeted." What she would discover was that he also had a high-tech camera, one designed by Flipper for marine purposes. However, it had proven effective at detecting objects underground, as well.

"Alright."

He heard the hope in her voice and figured that was because he'd shown interest in the dig site. She probably thought he was almost on board.

That wasn't the case. But he wouldn't tell her that yet.

When he didn't say anything else for a while, she lifted a brow and looked over at him. She even had a little smile on her face. That glow brightening her eyes almost undid him. "Any more questions, Gavin?"

There was something else; something he had to know. "Yes, but not about the dig. It's something about you that I want to know."

"What?" she asked, lifting an arched brow.

He held her gaze steadily. "When was the last time you made love with a man?"

Four

Layla gaped, certain Gavin hadn't asked her what she thought he'd asked her. What man would inquire that of a woman...especially one he'd known barely twenty-four hours? However, from the look on his face, he evidently saw nothing wrong with the question. He was sitting there waiting on an answer.

She lifted her chin and crossed her arms over her chest. When she saw his gaze shift from her eyes to her upraised breasts, she dropped her hands. "Do you actually expect me to answer that?" Somehow she managed to get the words past a constricted throat. The way he stared at her was making her head spin.

He shrugged massive broad shoulders. "Don't know why not. We're sexually attracted to each other. Just want to know what I'm dealing with when we decide to go for it and take the edge off."

Go for it? Take the edge off? Layla shook her head, clearly missing something. She knew they were attracted to each other; she got that. What she didn't get was him thinking that attraction meant they would eventually decide to "go for it." She had no intention of going anywhere. She was here to do a job and not indulge his fantasies…or her own, for that matter.

"I think you need to explain what exactly you're getting at. We agreed to keep sex out of this, Gavin."

"I didn't agree to any such thing. You suggested it but I didn't agree to it. Why would I?"

"Why wouldn't you?" she countered, not understanding his way of thinking.

He leaned back in his chair and her gaze watched his every movement. Restrained and controlled. She wondered if his actions were intentional, to put her off-kilter. When he picked up his glass of tea, her gaze automatically shifted to his hands. They were large and callous. They were the same hands that had sent shivers up her spine last night.

Memories of their kiss suddenly bombarded her and then her gaze shifted to his mouth as he took a swallow of iced tea. She was drawn to the way his mouth covered the rim of the glass and the way the liquid flowed down his throat. But what really got to her was the way he licked his lips afterward. When he caught her staring, those penetrating eyes darkened as they held hers.

"Want some?"

She snatched her gaze away. The lump in her throat thickened. She was glad to be sitting down; otherwise it would have been impossible to stand on both feet. The look he was giving her had her weak in the knees.

Somehow she managed to clear the lump in her throat and hold up her glass. "No thanks, I have my own."

His eyes blazed as they continued to hold hers. "I wasn't offering you any of my tea, Layla."

She sucked in a deep breath. He couldn't have set her straight any plainer than that. There was no need to ask what he was offering. That was the moment she knew Gavin Blake intended to be a problem. One she needed to deal with here and now.

"You never did answer my earlier question. When was the last time you were with a man?"

She set her glass of tea back down on the table. "And you never answered mine about why you wouldn't agree to keep sex out of it." Feeling flustered, she added, "We need to talk."

A smile touched the corners of his lips. "I thought that's what we were doing."

There was no way he could have thought that. What he was doing was deliberately getting her all unglued. If he thought for one minute his arrogant behavior would make her run, then he didn't know her very well. "There seems to be some sort of misunderstanding here."

"Is there?"

"Undoubtedly. I'm here to do a job…that is, if you let me stay to do it. But under no circumstances am I here for your pleasure, Gavin. I don't play those kinds of games. Evidently just because we shared a kiss last night, you've gotten the wrong idea about me. I need to set the record straight now. So hear me and hear me good." She leaned part of the way over the table toward him. Although his face was void of any expression, she was certain she had his undivided attention.

"I am *not* here to engage in an affair with you, if that's why you want to know about my sex life." *Or lack thereof.* But that was something he didn't need to know.

Gavin didn't say anything. He knew she assumed his attention was on her words. In truth his attention was on the mouth delivering those words. Her lips were perfectly shaped with a little cute dip in the center. He liked the play of that mutinous tip whenever she frowned and how those same lips folded pensively when she appeared in deep thought. But more than anything, he couldn't forget how those lips felt beneath his. Their lushness. How delicious they'd tasted. How sweet.

When she got quiet after delivering her spiel, he figured she thought she had set him straight. Far from it and it was time to let her know where he stood. "Are you finished?"

She seemed surprised by his question, but nodded nonetheless and said, "Yes, I'm finished."

She then straightened in her chair, her posture a lot more relaxed than it had been moments ago.

"Evidently, there's a lot you don't understand about sex, Layla."

Her body tensed again. And somehow those gorgeous lips looked even more sensual. "What's there to understand?" she asked.

Gavin continued to study her. He saw her nonchalant expression and noted her features had taken on a blasé look. Her apparent indifference to this discussion of sex could mean only one thing. She'd been cheated of something he considered as vital as breathing. Reaching her level of success in such a short period of time meant something had been sacrificed. An active sex life, perhaps?

"I want you and you want me," he said, deciding to point out the obvious.

"And?"

He forced himself not to smile, thinking she was pretending not to have a clue. Then it occurred to him that maybe she wasn't pretending. Maybe it was time to explain to her what it meant whenever a woman became the object of his personal fantasies.

"And…" he said, "we *will* sleep together."

She sat up in her chair, straightening her spine. Her lips went from sensual to tense but turned him on even more just the same. "No, we will not," she said adamantly.

He smiled. "Yes, we will. It's inevitable."

She frowned. "No, it's not. Just who do you think you are?"

He figured it was time she knew the answer to that. "A man who wants you. A man who intends to have you. A man who will show you, Layla Harris, just what you've been missing."

Layla tried to keep her heart from pounding deep in her chest, while at the same time fighting off the heat stroking through her body. She knew she shouldn't ask but she couldn't hold back.

"And just what do you think I've missed?"

"Hot, raunchy, mind-blowing sex. Evidently over the years you've been too preoccupied with other things to indulge. Don't you know it's not good to deprive your body of meeting certain needs?"

Her frown deepened. "I haven't deprived my body of anything."

"Haven't you? Why do you think you're so attracted to me?"

Layla actually rolled her eyes. Really? Honestly? Had he looked in the mirror lately? When was the last time he'd studied all those photos Ms. Melody had plastered on the walls. Any woman would be attracted to him. Even now he sat there not doing anything and still looked sexy as hell with that well-toned body of his. And here she was sitting across the table from him. Right within kissing distance.

As far as she was concerned, Gavin Blake was eye candy of the richest kind. Passion personified. But she definitely wouldn't tell him that. She would deny everything he'd said with her last breath if she had to.

"I am not all that attracted to you." At least she hadn't completely lied and said she wasn't attracted to him at all.

"You want me to prove otherwise?"

What was it with men always wanting to prove things when it came to sex? "No, thanks. That's not necessary."

"I think that it is."

He'd said the words in a low, vibrating tone

with a sexy rumble she wished she could ignore. But there was no way, what with all the shivers oozing down her spine. "Are you trying to scare me off, Gavin?"

He lifted a brow. "Scare you off?"

"Yes. Say all these things so I get angry enough to leave the ranch, sparing you the trouble of making a decision one way or the other about whether I can dig on your land or not."

"Is that what you think?"

To be honest, she didn't know what to think. She needed his land and all he had on his mind was sex. That made her wonder...

"Then are you trying to box me into a corner? Implying that I will have to sleep with you before you'll give me permission to dig?"

Gavin shook his head. "I would never put pressure on you to sleep with me. But be forewarned, Layla. If you hang around here doing that dig, we *will* sleep together. There's no way we won't. Your own body will betray you. When it does, I will be ready for the opportunity."

Seriously? If he thought her body would eventually weaken, he didn't know her. And that was the point, one she couldn't lose sight of. He *didn't* know her. He didn't know about her dedication when it came to her work. Nor did he know of her ability to be single-minded when it came to her career goals. She could put everything out of her mind except what was most important. She was driven to be successful in her field, and she wouldn't let Gavin—or any other man—stand in her way.

He was pretty sure of himself where women were concerned. A man couldn't look like him, be built like him, and not be in demand and get any woman he wanted. All Gavin had to do was snap his fingers and she figured the women came running. Being denied anything from a woman would be foreign to him.

"Think whatever you want, Gavin, but I'm not the kind of woman you're used to. I won't break."

He rubbed his hand over his chin as he studied her. "Would you want to bet on that?"

Layla frowned. She had no intention of betting on anything and she proceeded to tell him that. He only smiled, and it was one of those smiles she was getting to know too well. The one that made her body sizzle when it should make her angry. His smile all but said he had her where he wanted her.

"Would you be willing to bet on it to guarantee your dig on the Silver Spurs?"

That piqued her interest. "Depending on what you have in mind." She hoped she was not setting herself up for something she would regret.

Gavin held back his *gotcha* smile. Little did Layla know but his teammates didn't call him Viper for nothing. To some, a viper might be considered a spiteful or treacherous person, but for him the name meant he knew how to capture his prey using any means necessary. Striking when they least expected it. He wanted her in his bed willingly and he intended to do whatever it took to get her there. It was time to push his agenda.

"I'm willing to make a deal, Layla."

"What sort of a deal?" She held his gaze.

Did she know how beautiful her facial features were? How striking her bone structure? He could sit for hours and stare, taking her in. But doing so would make him want her even more than he already did. Before he'd met her, he couldn't have imagined that degree of need for any woman. But he could imagine it for her.

He lifted his shoulder in a half shrug as if what he was about to say wasn't of grave importance. As if he really didn't care one way or the other if she took the deal or left it on the table.

"I'm not as convinced about this buried loot as you and my grandmother seem to be," he said. "And I doubt reading any report will make me change my mind. But wanting you in my bed will," he said bluntly, needing her to fully understand what he was saying.

"This is the deal," he continued. "I will let you dig, regardless of what I think. If you find something, great. You will have proven me wrong. I will be happy for you. Be the first to congratulate you on a job well done. However, if you come up with nothing then you admit you want me as much as I want you and we sleep together."

"You are counting on me failing? And plan to take advantage of me if I do?"

The thought was firing her up. He could tell. The flash of fire in her eyes told it all. "You shouldn't worry about failing. Unless you think you will. If there's some doubt in your mind regarding the accuracy of your research, then I understand if—"

"My research is on point. There's no doubt in my mind about anything."

His smile spread across his lips. "In that case, do we have a deal?"

Five

At that moment Layla realized just what was going on. Whether it was his intent or not, Gavin was forcing her to believe in herself, to prove that she was right in her belief that Jesse James had buried treasure on Gavin's land.

"Well?"

The determination was clear in his eyes. He intended to sleep with her. She was just as determined that he wouldn't. She didn't like the deal he'd offered. In all honesty, she should be appalled by it. Instead she saw it as her chance to prove she was above the desire he couldn't stop talking about. She would find Jesse James's loot.

She had no doubts. There was no need getting irritated that he was a typical male who thought a good roll between the sheets was the answer to everything. She would never be able to convince him that when it came to sex, she had always been able to take it or leave it, no matter how tempting it was to indulge. He would find that out for himself.

She'd be free to run her dig and make the finding of not only her career but of a lifetime. She wouldn't think about the traitorous voice that said it might be nice to lose this bet and get the consolation prize…

"Fine."

He lifted his brow. "Does that mean you accept the deal?"

"As long as you give me your word you won't try to hinder me and my team in any way."

"I wouldn't do that."

Yeah. Right. There was no reason for her to trust he wouldn't do just about anything to make sure the result worked out in his favor. Another typical male trait. No man liked losing. "Whatever you say."

"You're going to have to trust me."

Layla rolled her eyes. "Sorry to disappoint you, but I don't know you enough to trust you."

"I can remedy that."

"Don't do me any favors." Layla eased out of her chair, feeling like she'd mentally run a marathon. "So will you give me your word as a SEAL that you won't try anything underhanded?"

"You think my word as a SEAL means something?"

"Yes. SEALs are a special team of men who take the job of protecting our country very seriously, and they live by a code of honor and integrity."

Gavin nodded. She was right. "And you know this how?"

"My father's cousin used to be a SEAL. He retired a few years ago, but he told us all about them. At least what he could share. A lot of the stuff he did was classified."

"The majority of our missions are," Gavin said.

"So, will you give me your word?"

"Yes, you have my word."

As far as Gavin was concerned, getting her into his bed before the dig began would not be interfering with the job she wanted to do.

"Good." She glanced at her watch. "It's getting late. I'm sure you need more sleep. However, if you need help with the dishes, then I—"

"No, I don't need help with the dishes. That's what dishwashers are for."

"Do you still want to see where we plan to dig?"

"Yes. I want to know what you have planned on my property and where."

"No problem."

"Then I'll come by the cottage in the morning," he said, standing, as well. "Come on. I'll walk you back."

She shook her head as she put on her sweater. "That's not necessary."

"It is for me, Layla. I'll walk you back."

She didn't deny him, maybe she didn't want to appear ungrateful. She headed for the door and when she reached out to open it, he moved his hand forward, as well. She didn't seem aware that he'd been standing so close behind her. His fingers closed over hers and his chest was flush against her back.

"I can open the door, Gavin," she said, glancing over her shoulder, obviously flustered at his nearness. He loomed over her five-foot-three-inch height. He stood so close he could smell her with every breath.

"Your choice." Releasing his hand from hers he eased back. She opened the door and inhaled the cool Missouri air.

"Nice night, isn't it?" he asked her. He walked beside her now.

"Yes, it is a nice night." She glanced over at him again. "Glad to be home?"

A smile touched his lips. "Yes. It's always good to be home. Time to go from SEAL to rancher."

"Is it that easy?"

"I'm used to it now. I have good men working for me who make the transition less difficult."

She nodded. "You love being a SEAL?"

"Yes."

"I understand your father and grandfather were SEALs."

Gavin wondered what else his grandmother had told her about their family. "Yes, they were SEALs. So I guess you can say it's in my blood.

What about your folks? Are they college professors like you?"

"No. They're both neurosurgeons. I didn't follow in their footsteps. Medicine didn't interest
me."

He hadn't asked her to explain, but the fact that
she did led him to believe her choice of a career
was a sore spot with someone. "You are your
own person, Layla." She was definitely her own
woman, he thought further to himself. "Just because following in my father's and grandfather's
footsteps worked for me, doesn't mean following
family tradition works for everybody."

She didn't say anything for a minute. "My parents wanted me to be a mini-them and go to medical school. But I couldn't. I'm not a healer. I'm
a historian."

"Then you did the right thing by following your
heart. When did you decide on archaeology?"
Gavin wondered if she noted how in sync their
steps were.

"In my junior year of high school." She paused
as if she was remembering. "My history teacher
had gone on an excavation in Egypt the summer
before and told us about it. I found it fascinating

how her team was able to dig up artifacts, how they found history buried beneath the earth's surface. It made me realize that's what I wanted to do."

"Why Jesse James?"

He heard her chuckle and the sound stimulated him in a way he wished it didn't. "Why *not* Jesse James?" He heard the amusement in her tone. "I used to watch Westerns with my grandfather whenever I visited him in New Orleans. He was a fan of the outlaw Jesse James. He read a lot of books about him. Watched movies and documentaries. I shared his love and interest. That's how my research began. And it's only grown over the years."

He heard the passion for her subject in her voice. It was there whenever she spoke about her work. She believed in it. If there had been any doubt in his mind before, there wasn't now. She would risk sleeping with him to prove her work.

She'd be disappointed not to find what she was searching for. But Gavin looked forward to helping her get over the disappointment. He didn't believe for one minute that James's loot was buried on this land. It wasn't. He recalled years ago when he'd been in high school, his father had given some outfit permission to check out the land because there was a chance of finding oil. They'd come up with nothing then, and he was certain Layla and her team would come up with nothing now.

"I guess this is where we need to say good-night."

They had reached the party house. Her words told him he wouldn't be invited inside. Maybe that was for the best. He doubted he could keep his hands off of her if they were behind closed doors. And regardless of what she thought, she wouldn't resist him. Last night's kiss had proven that. He wasn't worried about the outcome of the deal between them. Like he'd told her, eventually her body would betray her and she would break. What had happened in his grandmother's kitchen when their hands touched at the door was a prime example of the intensity of the desire between them.

"So what time do you want us to meet tomorrow?" she asked, reclaiming his attention.

"I need to ride out with Caldwell and my men

at the crack of dawn to check on a few things. I'll be back around ten. Will that time work for you?"

"Yes."

"Good. We can ride in my truck."

"Alright. Good night."

She turned toward the door, intent on opening it quickly and going inside. He was just as determined not to let her get away that easily. Reaching out, he wrapped his arms around her waist and tugged her close to him.

"What do you think you're doing, Gavin?"

"This."

Lowering his head, he claimed her mouth in a long, passionate kiss. She didn't push him away. Instead, she pulled him closer. Emotions he hadn't expected pushed him to let her know with this kiss just how much he wanted her.

The kiss they'd shared last night had been a game changer. This one sealed their fate.

Gavin knew at that moment that kissing her would never be enough. What he really wanted to do was sweep her off her feet, open the damn door and head straight to the bedroom. But he couldn't do that.

He wanted her to admit how much she wanted him, too. He'd give her time; he'd remember their deal. The one he had initiated. The one he intended to end in his favor. There was no way she would leave the Silver Spurs without them making love.

He finally broke off the kiss. As he drew in a deep breath he watched her draw in one, as well. Studying her mouth, he saw her lips were wet and swollen, and he had to fight back the urge to kiss her again.

"Why did you kiss me?" she asked, touching her finger to her lips.

He smiled, tempted to replace her finger with the tip of his tongue. "For the same reason you let me kiss you. I want you and you want me."

From the look he saw in her eyes, he knew she was angry. Why? Because he'd stated facts when she preferred hiding behind denials?

"I'm going inside now."

"I'll see you in the morning around ten."

She nodded, then quickly opened the door and went inside. When the door closed behind her, Gavin shoved his hands into the pockets of his jeans and headed back toward the main house.

He knew she was confused. Confusion came with the territory when you tried to deny the truth of your feelings. However, she was smart. He knew she would figure it out. Eventually she would see things the way he did.

He would make sure of it.

Six

Layla, feeling tousled from a restless night, stepped out on the porch with a cup of coffee in her hand. She took a sip. She needed the hot liquid as much as she needed more sleep. Kissing Gavin was hazardous to her health when the aftereffect was a frazzled mind.

What could she have been thinking to agree to the deal he'd put on the table? What woman in her right mind would agree to have sex with a man who counted on her to fail at the most important project of her life? She kept assuring herself that she had nothing to worry about because her research wasn't wrong.

But what if it was?

She shook her head, refusing to second-guess herself or allow something as insignificant as sex to undermine her confidence in years of research. She lifted the cup to her lips again, took another sip and smiled. She couldn't wait to show Gavin just how wrong he was. She would leave the Silver Spurs with Jesse James's loot *and* she'd keep Gavin out of her panties.

She glanced over at the main house and tried to ignore the heat that settled in her stomach. Ms. Melody had called to invite Layla to breakfast, but she'd declined saying she needed to read over a few reports. The last thing Layla wanted was to run into Gavin. She would see him at ten and that suited her just fine. The man had a way of making her distracted.

And then there was that kiss she couldn't stop thinking about. The one that still had her lips tingling this morning. While getting dressed she'd tried to convince herself not to worry about that kiss—not to worry about anything, especially not Gavin Blake. Agreeing to his deal meant nothing more than a reason to work harder to find James's stash. She hadn't lied to Ms. Melody. Layla had used this morning to review several documents.

It was important to make sure she hadn't missed anything in her research.

Layla checked her watch. Gavin would be arriving in an hour. That wasn't a lot of time to prepare to see him again. But then she doubted she would ever be prepared for the likes of Gavin Blake.

"So what have you decided about the dig, Gavin?"

Gavin glanced up from his breakfast plate and met his grandmother's eyes. He'd been in bed when she'd returned last night, but there was no getting out of the conversation this morning. One thing was for certain, he would not tell her about the deal he'd struck with Layla.

"Layla is showing me the site this morning. I want to check it out for myself before I make a decision." He then resumed eating, hoping to end the conversation.

"So when are you leaving for Mississippi?"

He looked up at his grandmother again with a raised brow. "Who said anything about me going to Mississippi?"

She lifted her own brow. "Yesterday you mentioned you had important business to take care of there."

Now he recalled mentioning it. "I changed my mind and won't be leaving after all." He resumed eating again, knowing his grandmother was eyeing him suspiciously.

"Why?"

He lifted his head again. "Why, what?"

"Why are you hanging around here?"

He held her inquisitive gaze. "Do you have a problem with me hanging around here, Gramma Mel?"

"Not as long as you don't have some shenanigans brewing in that head of yours, Gavin."

If only you knew, he thought. He pushed his plate away. "Breakfast was good as usual. I'm surprised you didn't invite Layla to join us."

"I did. But she made an excuse for not coming. I wonder why."

He stood. His grandmother was fishing for information and he was determined not to get caught. "I have a call with Phil to go over the books. I'll be in my office for an hour or so."

"Alright. And you may have changed your mind about going to Mississippi, but I'm still scheduled to go to that library conference in Cincinnati. It lasts a week, and I booked it before I knew you were coming home."

Gavin knew his grandmother enjoyed going to those conferences. "You should go," he encouraged.

She looked at him as if he wasn't trustworthy... of all things. "Is anything wrong?" he asked her.

"You tell me, Gavin. You're not fooling me one bit. I know that look. You're up to something and whatever it is, I hope you don't get caught in your own trap."

"What trap?"

"I'll let you figure that one out. But keep something in mind."

He lifted a brow. "What?"

"Layla is not Jamie."

He frowned deeply. "What is that supposed to mean?"

"It means I think something good could develop between the two of you, if you let it. But you won't. You're afraid she will be like Jamie. Whether you choose to believe me or not, your mom loved you and your dad. I would sit and hear her crying for him at night when he was gone."

"Then why did she leave?"

"Loneliness drove her away, Gavin. The Silver Spurs isn't meant for everyone and she was miserable here. Not everyone can handle the isolation."

"But that was no reason for her to desert me and Dad."

Without saying anything else he turned and walked out of the kitchen toward his office.

A lump formed in Layla's throat when she heard the knock at the door. She didn't have to look out of the peephole to see who it was. Gavin had said he would arrive at ten and it was ten on the dot. She glanced down at herself and then wished she hadn't. Why should she care what he thought about how she looked today? And why had she decided to wear her hair down instead of back in a ponytail?

She opened the door and Gavin stood leaning in the doorway. He filled the space, looking like he needed to be some woman's breakfast, lunch and dinner. Why did the man have to be so over-the-top gorgeous? Why did she want to drool, drool, and then drool some more?

And why did she want to snatch him inside and have her way with him?

She had no right to think any of those things, no right to fantasize. She had to stay focused on her work. "Good morning. I'm ready," she said, grabbing her jacket. He moved aside when she stepped out and closed the door behind herself.

"Good morning, Layla. I hope you slept well," Gavin said as they walked off the porch.

He slid his hand to her elbow to help her down the steps and she wished he hadn't. Immediately, a spike of desire shot through her and she was tempted to snatch her arm away.

"Nice day, isn't it?"

"Yes, it's nice." She glanced over at him as he kept his hand on her elbow while he led her to his truck and opened the door.

"And speaking of nice," he said, gripping her elbow a little tighter as he helped her up into the passenger seat. "You look good this morning. Real nice."

"Thank you."

He closed the truck door and as she watched

him move around the front of the truck to the driver's side, she couldn't help thinking that he looked pretty good himself. Real nice. A pair of jeans hugged masculine thighs, a pullover sweater and a leather bomber jacket with the crest of a SEAL on the back graced broad shoulders. In her book there was something about a man who wore a leather bomber jacket, whether he was a biker, a model or a navy SEAL.

She kept her gaze trained on him. When he opened the door and slid onto the leather seat, she couldn't help but appreciate how the fit of his jeans tightened on his thighs.

"You went riding around your ranch dressed like that?"

"No. We finished early so I had time to change before joining my grandmother for breakfast. She missed your presence at breakfast by the way."

"I told her about the report I had to review this morning."

He didn't say anything and she wondered if he believed her.

"You okay?"

It was only then that she realized she was still staring. She snatched her gaze away from his thighs, regretting that he'd caught her ogling him. "I'm fine."

A smile curved his lips and her insides felt like they'd turned to mush. "Just checking," he said, snapping his seat belt in place. "I don't want you to start admitting you want me anytime soon."

Layla frowned, remembering what he'd said last night. "Trust me. That won't be happening." She spoke with a degree of confidence she wasn't feeling, especially when he shifted gears, causing those thighs to catch her attention again.

She forced her gaze out the window to view the pastures, valleys and hills they passed. Not for the first time, she thought the Silver Spurs was beautiful. Already they'd passed the new barn and several other smaller buildings. And there were several fenced rolling plains filled with cows. The sun peeked through a bevy of trees that layered the countryside and she knew it would be a beautiful day even with the chill in the air.

"Sleep well?"

She glanced over at him, wondering why he would ask. Did he assume that she hadn't? Well, she intended to crush that assumption right then and there. "Yes, like a baby, straight through the night." Maybe she'd laid it on too thick since most babies didn't sleep straight through the night.

"Glad to hear it. So did I. I slept so well that I almost overslept this morning." He didn't say anything for a minute. "Which way?"

She lifted a brow. "What?"

"Directions. Gramma Mel said the spot is just past the old barn. Which way do I go after that?"

The barn he was talking about was a big empty building painted red. According to Ms. Melody, it hadn't been used in years but the structure looked sound. More than once Layla had been tempted to take a peek inside but the doors were bolted up. She wondered if Gavin would allow them to keep their excavation equipment stored there. Since he seemed in a pretty good mood this morning, it might be a good time to ask. "And about that old barn?"

"What about it?"

"I'm going to need a place to store my heavy equipment, like the loader backhoe and tractor, for the excavation. May I use the old barn?"

He glanced over at her and she could imagine what he was thinking. Why should he do anything to help her when he was counting on her to fail? He surprised her when he said, "Yes, you can use the old barn."

She smiled. Since he was being so generous she decided to go for the gusto. "There's also a smaller building next to the barn. I understand it used to be the old bunkhouse."

"What about it?"

"May I use that, as well? I'll need somewhere to test soil samples and such."

He looked at her again. "Are you trying to take advantage of my kindness, Layla?"

"Yes, I guess I am, Gavin."

A husky chuckle escaped his lips. "At least you're honest. Yes, you can use that old shack, as well."

"Thank you."

"You're welcome."

She didn't say anything for a minute as they drove. "Make a left turn at the next tree and drive another couple of miles," she said. "You can park in the clearing next to the stumps. I've marked the exact spot where we'll be digging."

"Okay."

The rest of the drive was done in silence. She

was glad when he finally brought the truck to a stop a short while later.

Gavin drew in a deep breath. With his hands still gripping the steering wheel he stared straight ahead at the view out of the windshield. He needed to get his bearings. Everything about Layla was getting to him. The way she looked, her scent, the way she wore her hair. The way that same hair had blown in the wind when his truck whooshed across his property.

"I can tell you miss coming here."

Did she make that assumption because of the way he was still sitting here, trying to keep his mind and body under control? Yet, she was right. He had missed coming here.

"Yes. As a kid I used to come to this area a lot. There's a huge lake not far from here. It separates our land from the Lotts' property and it's on the Lotts' land. But that didn't mean anything to me. Not even the no-swimming-allowed sign Sherman Lott had posted. I used to sneak into the lake and go swimming as a teen every chance I got. On a good day I would swim for hours without getting caught."

"And on a bad day?"

He chuckled. "On a bad day Sherman Lott would call my grandmother and report me for trespassing."

She lifted a brow. "Honestly? He would actually call and tell on you?"

"All the time. He didn't like anyone swimming or fishing in that lake. But I had a lot of years of good fishing there, as well."

He smiled, remembering how defying Mr. Lott had pleased him immensely. "Time to look around. But before we get out there's something we need to do."

She lifted her brow. "What?"

"Kiss. More than anything, I want to kiss you, Layla."

Layla couldn't believe he'd said that. Kiss? Hadn't they done that enough already? Not that she was counting but he'd kissed her twice. Why was he going for three? Why was she hoping that he would?

"Kiss me?" she asked, softly, hoping he didn't pick up on the yearning in her voice.

"Yes, kiss you. It's either that or talk you into my truck's backseat."

She nibbled on her bottom lip. "And you think doing that will be easy?"

"No, but it will be worth all the effort I plan to put into it. So how about unbuckling that seat belt and leaning a little over here? I promise it will be painless."

Being painless, Layla thought, was the least of her worries. "Haven't you gotten enough? Of kissing me?" she asked, studying the look in his eyes.

"No, I haven't gotten enough, so lean over this way. Let's engage in something pleasurable."

The urgency in his voice was so intense, it sent shivers through her. She knew they shouldn't kiss again. Doing so would lead to assumptions on his part that she'd rather he not have. But she'd had a hard time forgetting how pleasurable their last two kisses had been. Both times his tongue had stroked hers to a feverish pitch, until she had greedily responded.

Frustration spilled from her lungs in a sigh and with very little control left, she unsnapped her seat belt and leaned closer to him. In spite of her misgivings, she was prepared to give him the kiss he wanted because it was a kiss she wanted, as well.

He leaned in to meet her and their lips touched. On her breathless sigh, he slid his tongue inside her mouth and began mating with her tongue. She felt his intensity all the way to her toes.

She wrapped her arms around his neck as he wrapped his arms around her waist. They were sitting in his truck, kissing like oversexed teenagers. Like they had nothing better to do and all day to do it. How crazy was that? But the insanity was lost as she tasted him. He tasted primitive, untamed and wild with lust. How could she detect such a thing in a kiss? Was this a warning that she should back off? That Gavin Blake would be the one man she couldn't ignore?

The latter gave her pause, but not enough to stop her tongue from mingling with his. Not enough to refrain from following his lead when he deepened the kiss. Not enough to stop the moan escaping her throat.

Layla knew then that she was a goner.

Seven

Gavin greedily devoured Layla's mouth. Never before had any woman escalated his arousal to such a state. And never had any woman made him want to kiss her each and every time he saw her.

Every bone and muscle in his body throbbed with a need for her that went beyond desire. Intense heat curled inside of him, threatening his control. And the one thing he was known for was control. So why were his brain cells faltering under the onslaught of such a delicious kiss? Why was his body making urgent demands for him to make love to her right here in his truck? Damn. What could he say?

Nothing. He was totally at a loss for words, which was a good thing since he didn't have time to indulge in any. He preferred using his mouth for this kiss. He intended to get his fill. But a part of him wasn't sure he could ever get his fill of Layla. He saw her and he wanted her. That wasn't good. He had to get control of his body and of the situation. And he needed to do so now.

Gavin reluctantly broke off the kiss. Drawing his mouth away from hers was one of the hardest things he'd had to do. He saw the look of denied need in her eyes before she leaned back, dropped her head against the headrest and closed her eyes. He figured she was as in awe of what just happened as he was.

What they'd shared wasn't just a kiss. It was an acknowledgment of deep sexual desires. He knew what was driving his and he thought he had figured out what was driving hers. She just refused to accept it. She was stubborn. It would take a lot more kisses like this one to bring her around. They'd felt an intense attraction to each other from the first, and from all appearances, things had gotten worse.

He continued to stare at her as heat curled inside of him. He wanted her. Bad. And that pushed him to say, "So tell me again why we can't sleep together."

Layla heard his words but she couldn't respond. Neither could she open her eyes to look at him. There was no point. She knew what she would see in the depths of his dark gaze. A sexual need so hot it was likely to sizzle her insides. It would make her fully aware of her own sexual need. A need he stirred to life inside her whether she wanted him to or not.

"Open your eyes, Layla. I'm not going anywhere."

At least not today. She suddenly remembered Ms. Melody mentioning he had to go to Mississippi on business. "When are you leaving?" she asked, opening her eyes.

Just as she'd expected. The eyes staring at her were dark and seductive.

He lifted a brow. "Leaving for where?"

"Mississippi. Your grandmother mentioned you had important business to take care of there."

"Trying to get rid of me, are you?"

"It wouldn't hurt," she said and saw his eyes

get even darker when she moistened her bottom lip with the tip of her tongue. "So when are you leaving?"

He moved his gaze from her mouth to her eyes. "I changed my mind about Mississippi. I'm not leaving here any time soon." She couldn't stop the disappointment that flashed through her.

"But I thought you had important business to take care of."

"My plans have changed. Do you have a problem with that?"

"I just hope you don't plan to get underfoot."

"I'll try not to. Now show me the exact spot where you plan to dig," he said, opening the truck door to get out.

No matter what he said, Layla knew Gavin would try getting underfoot.

When Gavin pulled an odd-looking camera from his backseat, Layla lifted a brow. "What is that?"

He smiled. "A Vericon 12D. It's a high-tech camera that's mainly used underwater. Flipper messed around with it so we could use it on land, as well."

"Flipper?"

"Yes, Flipper. One of my team members. He's into technology and all that high-tech stuff," Gavin said as they walked side by side.

"Surely Flipper isn't his real name."

Gavin chuckled. "His real name is David Holloway. His code name is Flipper."

"Oh," she said, glancing up at him. "Do you have a code name?"

"Yes."

"What is it?"

He saw no reason not to tell her since his grandmother was well aware of it, too. His teammates called Gavin by his code name whenever they came to visit. "Viper."

Layla scrunched up her features. "Viper?"

"Yes, Viper."

"Why?"

"Why what?"

"Why do they call you Viper?"

He stopped walking to answer her, and when he stopped, she did, too. He hadn't noticed before how small she seemed, standing close to him. He figured he'd never noticed because usually when he faced her he was fixated on her mouth.

"The reason I'm called Viper is because when I set my sights on a target, I don't give up until I make a hit. I love taking the enemy down."

She tilted her head to look up at him. "Do you consider me an enemy?"

He didn't hesitate. "No." She wasn't the enemy, but he had every intention of taking her down... right into his bed.

Evidently satisfied with his response, she looked around him, back toward where the truck was parked. Then she turned around. She did it several times and each time he saw her confusion deepen.

"Is something wrong?" he finally asked.

She whipped around to look at him. "Yes, something is wrong."

He glanced around before returning his gaze to her. "What?"

"Someone moved my marker. It's gone."

He lifted a brow. "What do you mean your marker is gone?"

She frowned. "Just what I said. Someone moved my marker. It's not here."

Gavin released a deep sigh. "Why would anyone move your marker? Are you sure you put one down?"

"Of course I'm sure," she answered in an annoyed tone. "Someone moved it."

Gavin raised his gaze upward. "And who would do that?"

"I don't know, but someone did."

He shook his head. "Layla, the Silver Spurs is out in the middle of nowhere. And this particular spot is considered way outside our working area, almost six miles from the main house. No one would deliberately come on this land to remove your marker."

"Well, someone did, Gavin. I marked the digging site," she said with deep irritation in her voice.

Gavin stared down at her. "Are you sure? Maybe your mind is clouded right now. I can understand my kiss leaving you that way."

Her frown deepened. "I'm serious, Gavin."

"So am I, Layla."

Exasperation darkened her expression. "Will you get your mind off sex for a minute?"

A smile touched his lips. "My mind wasn't on sex," he said. "It was on that kiss we shared. But

since you've pulled sex into the conversation…
it's hard to think of anything other than getting
you in my bed when you look so good."

Layla pushed to the back of her mind that she'd
deliberately taken more time with her appearance
just so he would think she looked good. That was
before she'd come out here and discovered her
marker *had* been removed.

"You moved it, didn't you?" she asked with an
accusing glare.

"Now why would I want to do that?"

When she didn't say anything but continued to
stare at him, his amusement was replaced with a
deep frown. "I have no reason to mess with any
marker you claim to have put down. This is the
first time I've been out this far from the house
since returning home."

He rubbed a hand down his face in frustration.
"If that marker has in fact been removed, then
that means someone trespassed on this land to
do it. Although for the life of me I can't imagine who would have cared enough to do such a
thing. I just think you're confused as to where
you placed the damn marker," he said, glancing

around. "The south pasture is rather large. Maybe it's all the way on the other side."

"I am not confused and it's not on the other side. Not only did I map its coordinates, I recall parking near those tree stumps and walking twenty to thirty feet to my right. The marker was a wooden stake with a red flag on it, and I planted it exactly where we would dig."

"If you're sure of that, then you need to consider who knows you're here. And who would want to see you fail."

She lifted her chin. "And why wouldn't your name head the list? The deal we agreed on means I would have to sleep with you if I fail."

Gavin took a step closer to her. "Whether you fail or succeed means nothing to me because I have every intention of sleeping with you regardless of the outcome of this dig."

Layla was taken aback by Gavin's words. Of all the audacity. She placed her hands on her hips. Anger poured through her. "And how do you figure that?"

"Because, like I explained to you earlier, I'm Viper. I set my sights on a target. I don't give up until I make a hit. You are my target, Layla, and I plan to break down your resolve."

She all but stomped her foot in frustration. "And I've told you that won't happen. What part of that don't you understand?"

"This part," he said, brushing his finger across her cheek. She couldn't downplay her sharp intake of breath or the way her body shuddered beneath his touch. "You do something to me and I do something to you," he continued. "We do things to each other. We can only hold out for so long."

She tilted her lips stubbornly. "I will fight you on that with my last breath."

"And I suggest you save that breath for that explosive orgasm you're going to have."

Layla opened her mouth to blast out a resounding retort but then she closed it without responding. What was the use of arguing with him about something she knew for a fact wouldn't be happening, no matter what he thought? So what if his touch warmed her to the core? She would put him out of her mind. She had more important things to be concerned with. Like who'd removed her marker and why. No matter what Gavin might assume, she was not imagining things.

"My marker was removed, Gavin."

He rolled his eyes. "We're back to that again?"

"Yes. The dig is why I'm here. Why I crazily agreed to your deal. If you didn't remove the marker, then who did?"

Gavin drew in a deep breath, trying to hold his aggravation and frustration at bay. He knew for certain she was not incompetent. So someone had removed the marker like she claimed.

"Here, hold this," he said, handing Flipper's camera to her. He then began walking, studying the ground. He slowed when he saw footprints he knew weren't hers or his. He crouched down and pressed his finger to one, touching the indention in the earth. It was cold. The tracks looked fresh, as if they hadn't been made any more than forty-eight hours ago. Whose prints were they? One of his men? Possibly, but for some reason he doubted it. All his men had been working in the north and west pastures for the past few days. None had any reason to come to the south pasture.

It appeared more weight had been placed on the left leg as that impression was deeper. He also noted the sole of the right shoe appeared more worn than the left.

He stood and backtracked to where Layla said she'd parked her vehicle when she'd come out here. He walked, looking down and around the entire time. When he'd gone about thirty feet he stopped. Crouching down again he studied the earth and that's when he saw the small plug where the marker had been. He glanced to the right and the left, studying the ground. Again he saw footprints. The same ones.

He stood and slowly walked back to Layla. Without saying anything, he took the camera out of her hand. "Thanks."

She raised a brow. "Well?"

She hadn't asked what he'd been doing. She was smart enough to figure things out. He was using his skill as a SEAL to determine if there was proof that the marker had been removed.

He met her inquisitive expression. "I saw footprints. I also saw where the marker had been. You're right. The marker was removed."

"Why? By whom?"

"Don't know, Layla." He honestly didn't have a clue. The Silver Spurs was private property. And although there were numerous ways to get on the property, he couldn't imagine anyone having a reason to come to this particular area. The one thing he didn't see was tire tracks. But the person could have parked elsewhere and walked.

"I planned on using this camera to scan the area," he said. "I suggest you make a list of anyone who might have a reason for wanting you not to succeed in your dig. And make sure you take me off the list. I told you my position and I'm sticking to it."

And without saying anything else, he walked off.

Eight

I told you my position and I'm sticking to it.

Later that day, Layla paced the floor. Gavin Blake was bullheaded, stubborn and full of himself. He was crazy if he actually thought he could get her to bend to his will. No way. No how. So why was she pacing the floor, wearing out both herself and her shoes?

She had watched him use that high-tech camera, but she hadn't been impressed with his findings. Gavin agreed there was something buried in the area but he refused to consider it was Jesse James's loot. To his way of thinking, since that area used to be a popular hunting spot, the camera had picked up nothing more than buried bullet shells.

Layla refused to believe her research was wrong. There was buried treasure somewhere in the south pasture, she was sure of it. And as far as who would not want to see her succeed in this project, that could be a number of people, including her parents. But she didn't for one minute think they would go so far as to sabotage the dig site. They were hoping failing at this would make Layla realize she should pursue medical school, after all. Then there was her older colleague Dr. Clayburn and others at the university who felt she'd been too young and inexperienced for such an expensive project. Did the person who removed the marker actually think she wouldn't have kept the coordinates and just re-marked it? That she would give up so easily?

She stopped pacing when she heard a knock on the door. The tightening in her stomach told her who it was. Why was Gavin here? She had spoken to Ms. Melody an hour or so ago when she'd called to invite Layla to dinner. Layla had regretfully declined, knowing she would not have been the best of company this evening. Besides, she needed distance from Gavin. Evidently he hadn't taken the hint.

The knock on the door sounded again. There was no need to pretend she wasn't there when Gavin knew she was. Crossing the room, she opened the door to find Gavin with a tray of food in his hand.

"After you told Gramma Mel you weren't coming to dinner, she strongly suggested I bring you something. I believe she thinks I'm the reason you didn't come to breakfast or dinner."

Layla moved aside to let him in. Tray and all. Especially the tray. Everything was covered but the food smelled good. "I'll let her know that's not the case when I talk to her tomorrow." No need for him to know he *had* been a factor in her decision.

"She might not be here. Not sure when she's leaving, whether it's tomorrow or the day after."

Layla closed the door and followed him to the kitchen. "Leaving? Ms. Melody is going somewhere?"

"Yes, to a library convention in Cincinnati for a week. But I'm sure she won't leave without saying goodbye. And if you expect me to take her place and make sure you don't miss meals…that won't be happening."

She frowned. "I never asked your grandmother to cook for me, Gavin."

He put the tray on the kitchen table and turned to her. "Don't you think I know that?"

"Then why did you insinuate otherwise?"

"Did I?"

She crossed her arms over her chest. "Yes, you did."

"Then I apologize." She couldn't help noticing how his gaze roamed over her. "You changed clothes," he said.

Was that disappointment she heard in his voice? Seeing his gaze had moved to her chest, she dropped her hands to her sides. "I showered."

"I know. You smell good. And you look good in that dress. Nice legs."

She would have appreciated the compliment if she wasn't still so uptight about that marker being moved. "I want to go back out to the dig site tomorrow and look around, Gavin. This time I want to use my own detector."

"If you're still concerned about why the marker was moved, I might have a reason for that."

She came into the kitchen, trying to ignore the way he was checking out her legs and the way her nipples responded to his blatant appraisal. "What reason is that?"

"Clete. He's an older man we hired years ago to keep the grounds clear of trash and debris as well as repair anything that needs fixing. That way Caldwell and the men can concentrate mainly on the cattle. When I mentioned the marker to Gramma Mel, she reminded me that Clete has a tendency to move stuff when he's keeping the land cleared."

"But why would he remove the marker?"

Gavin shrugged. "He probably didn't know what it was and thought it was trash. He and his wife left a few days ago to visit their son who is in the navy and stationed in Hawaii. I'll talk to him when he gets back."

Layla drew in a deep breath, feeling somewhat relieved. The thought of someone tampering with the dig site had definitely bothered her.

"Sit down and eat. I promised Gramma Mel that I would make sure you did."

She raised a suspicious eye. "Why?"

"Why what?"

"Why would you care one way or the other if I eat?"

A slow, sexy smile touched his lips and her womb seemed to contract with the weight of that smile. And his dimples had bone-melting fire spreading through her blood. "The reason I care is because I don't want you to start losing weight."

She crossed her arms over her chest again, and then quickly dropped them by her sides when she saw his gaze shift back to her chest. Could the man think of anything other than sex for a minute? "And what does my weight have to do with you?"

"When I make love to you, I want to feel meat on your bones."

His statement answered her earlier question. No, he obviously couldn't think of anything other than sex. "We won't be making love, Gavin."

"Your food is getting cold."

He was blatantly ignoring what she'd said. "I'll eat after you leave."

He chuckled. "If that was a hint that you want me to go, forget it. I want to make sure you eat."

She frowned. "What do you plan to do? Stay here and watch me."

"Yes, that was my intent."

He was serious. "I don't need a babysitter, Gavin."

"No. What you need is a lover, Layla. And you never did answer my question from last night. When was the last time you made love with a man?"

"And I don't intend to answer it because it's none of your business."

If he insisted on staying, she would ignore him. She moved to the table where he'd placed her food. Her mouth began watering the moment she uncovered it. Fried chicken, mashed potatoes, broccoli, candied yams and iced tea. And a slice of chocolate cake for dessert.

A smile lit her face. "Your grandmother is something else." Layla walked over to the sink to wash her hands. After grabbing utensils out of a drawer, she returned to the table and found Gavin sitting there. Did he plan to actually watch her eat? Didn't he have anything better to do?

Deciding nothing would stand between her and that food, she sat down, bowed her head and said grace, determined to ignore him. When she slid a forkful of mashed potatoes between her lips, she closed her eyes and groaned. Delicious.

"If you get off eating mashed potatoes, I can only imagine your reaction when we make love."

A part of her wanted to claim she wouldn't enjoy it. She quickly dismissed the idea when she glanced over at him. A woman could climax just from staring at him. Even so, she said, "In your dreams."

"My dreams will one day become your reality, Layla."

She decided not to argue with him anymore. But if he was intent on watching her, she might as well ask him a few questions. Get him talking, so she wouldn't think about how good he looked sitting there. How sexy.

She took a sip of her tea. "You mentioned your teammate named Flipper. Any others you're close to?"

"I'm close to all of them. We're a team."

"How many?"

"Enough."

She rolled her eyes. Had she asked about classified information or something? "I'm sure you're closer to some of the guys more than others."

He leaned back in the chair as if getting comfortable. She couldn't recall the last time she'd shared a private, intimate dinner with a man. And, whether she liked admitting it or not, this *was* intimate. They were alone, sitting at a table with the backdrop of a blazing fire roaring in the fireplace.

"In that case, I would say Flipper, Bane, Coop, Mac and Nick. The six of us went through all phases of training together. A couple of years ago, Nick took a job with Homeland Security. He needed a little more stability in his life when his wife gave birth to triplets."

As if he felt right at home, he stood and went to the refrigerator to get a beer and then returned to his chair. "Bane is a master sniper," he continued, popping the cap. "Coop is the mastermind behind most of our strategic moves. Mac is slightly older than the rest of us and likes to think he can keep us in line most of the time. He's been married for ages, has four kids and likes to impose his words of wisdom on us whether we want to hear them or not. And Flip can hold his breath under water longer than any human I know." He chuckled as he took a swig. "We're convinced Flipper has gills hidden somewhere."

Layla heard the fondness in his voice when he spoke of his teammates. "What's a master sniper?"

He looked at her. She thought he would say she was asking for classified information but then he said, "A master sniper is the best shot on the team. Bane is one badass. He can hit a target with one eye closed. He's covered all our backs more than once." He paused. "Bane and his wife, Crystal, are renewing their vows next month."

"Oh, were he and his wife separated for a while or something?"

"Yes, you could say that."

Layla knew he was being elusive but she was getting used to it. She didn't have to ask if his job was dangerous. Anyone who knew of the navy SEALs was aware of the types of missions they went on. She finished the rest of her meal in silence, with him watching her. She was tempted to ask if he wanted some but knew the trouble she'd gotten into when she'd asked him that question the last time.

She took a sip of her iced tea and looked over at him when she pushed her plate aside. "Satisfied, Gavin?"

He gave her a crooked smile. "Baby, my satisfaction will come when I get inside of you."

The glass nearly slipped from her hand. She recovered long enough to set it down by the plate. The impact of his words had her burning from the inside out. "Why do you say such things?"

"Just keeping it honest."

Gavin liked rattling Layla. Evidently she wasn't used to a man talking to her this way, telling her what he wanted and how he planned to make her feel. While watching her eat, his imagination had run wild. The conversation hadn't distracted him enough to demolish his desire. He doubted that was possible. He wanted her. He'd made that point pretty damn clear and he knew she wanted him as well, so what was the holdup?

"I've finished eating so you can leave now."

He held her gaze, felt the flare of response in their bodies when they looked at each other. Giving in to temptation, he lightly traced his fingertips along her arm. He felt her shiver beneath his touch. He heard her sharp intake of breath. "Why are you fighting this, Layla?"

"And why are you being so persistent?"

He could tell her that one of the reasons was because he hadn't been with a woman in six months, eight days, twelve hours and no telling how many minutes. Being around her was taking its toll. However, telling her such a thing would make him sound like a greedy jerk with only sex on his mind. That was only partly true. The other part was that he found her as fascinating as he found her beautiful.

"Being persistent is part of my nature."

When he saw her lips form a frown, his groin hardened and he couldn't help drawing in a ragged breath. Standing, he said, "I'll leave you alone now and report to Gramma Mel that you ate all your food."

He reached to remove the tray, but she blocked him. "Surely you don't think I'll let you return with dirty dishes."

"We've had a conversation about the purpose of a dishwasher before, Layla."

"That might be your way of doing things but it's not mine. I will wash the dishes and return them to Ms. Melody tomorrow," she said, standing.

Doing so brought her right smack in front of him. Gavin knew that if she inched closer, she would feel his erection. Even so, he intended to kiss her before he left.

"Walk me to the door, Layla."

From the look in her eyes, he knew she was aware of his plan. He watched her nibble her bottom lip. "Relax, baby. I won't bite."

She stopped nibbling her lips long enough to lift her chin and stare into his eyes. "You'll do something even worse, Gavin."

"What is that?"

"You will make me want you."

He eased closer, pressing his body to hers, wanting her to feel his erection. There was no way she could miss it. "Welcome to the club. And you already want me, Layla. Why are you having a hard time accepting that?"

Gavin could tell she was at a loss for words, which suited him just fine. He had other uses for her mouth. He leaned in to capture her lips.

* * *

Why was she having such a hard time accepting this? Layla asked herself when Gavin took her mouth. She didn't resist. She couldn't. In fact she felt herself practically melting into his arms. That was why, she reasoned, she wrapped her arms around his neck. Otherwise she would become a puddle on the floor.

He kissed her with an intensity she reciprocated in every part of her body. His mouth locked onto hers, not leaving any part of her mouth untouched. He tapped into areas she hadn't known existed. He was staking his claim on her mouth in a scandalous way. It was as if he was intentionally making her crazy for his kiss.

And then there was the feel of his erection, pressing hard against her middle. What man could get *that* aroused? To know she was the cause sent heated shivers through her body. The hard tips of her breasts pressed through the material of her dress as if eager to make contact with his chest.

Gavin broke off the kiss and when Layla drew in a deep breath, she was swept off her feet into his arms. He sat back down at the table with her firmly planted in his lap. Before she could ask just what he thought he was doing, his mouth was on hers. And just like before, this kiss robbed her of her senses, made her purr deep in her throat. It was a good thing his arm gripped her tightly otherwise she would topple to the floor. His hand was on her thigh, slowly caressing her skin underneath her dress.

Maybe she needed to ask herself why she was letting him do such a thing when she'd never let any man take such liberties before. Hadn't she kicked Sonny Paul in the groin when he thought he could reach into her blouse and touch her breast? Why did she believe this was different? Just because Gavin's mouth was driving her crazy with lust—could she accept this as okay?

And why was she still clutching him around the neck as if her life depended on their mouths being so intimately locked? Red-hot passion was making her dazed.

Somewhere in the haziness of her mind, she noted he had stood, without their mouths disconnecting. He was moving, headed somewhere rather quickly. It was only when he placed her on the bed that she regained her senses. Snatching her mouth from his, she scrambled away from him.

She blinked upon seeing he was about to take off his shirt. "What do you think you're doing?"

He stared down at her, panting like he'd run a marathon. His eyes, she saw, were glazed with heated lust to such a degree it made her heart pound. "About to make love to you, Layla." He then whipped his shirt over his head.

Seeing him bare chested caused goose bumps to ripple all over her skin. She scrambled farther away from him. "No you're not!"

He stared at her. "Can you look at me and say you don't want me to make love to you?"

She nervously licked her bottom lip and looked away. Yes, she could say it but she couldn't look at him while doing so. Mainly because she *did* want him to make love to her. There was no doubt in her mind that the sheets on the bed were calling their names.

"Layla. Look at me."

No, she wouldn't look at him. Nor would she tell him anything. Scrambling off the bed, she stood and began straightening her clothes before quickly walking out of the bedroom. "I'm showing you the door, Gavin," she called over her shoulder.

Once she reached the door, she waited. It took him a few minutes to follow her. He probably needed time to put his shirt back on and get his lusty mind under control.

When she saw him walking toward her he had an unreadable expression on his face. She drew in a deep breath. What thoughts were going through his mind? Did he think she was nothing more than a tease because she'd stoked his fire and then doused it with water? She would admit to having gotten caught up in the moment like he had. However, although he was ready to take things to the next level, she was not.

When he got closer, she saw the way he stared at her and figured he was angry to the point that he would walk out the door without saying anything to her.

She figured wrong. When Gavin stopped before opening the door, he turned dark, livid eyes on her. He then said in a furious voice, "The next time we kiss, Layla, will be when we make love. It's going to be a package deal."

He then opened the door and left.

Nine

Late afternoon the next day, Gavin walked out on the porch with a steaming cup of coffee. He couldn't believe he'd jogged around the ranch house twenty times last night. That would be equivalent to ten miles. When was the last time he'd done that?

On top of his workout last night, he'd gotten up at the crack of dawn to ride the range with Caldwell and his men. Sharing breakfast with them over an open fire had brought back memories. Most of the men who worked for Gavin had worked for his dad and had known Gavin when he'd been a kid. Although they called him boss, he knew they did it out of respect and not because he was involved in the day-to-day operations. Caldwell took care of the place. No matter how long Gavin was away from the ranch, he rested easy at night knowing the Silver Spurs was in good hands. Gavin also knew that whenever he returned Caldwell had no problem relinquishing that leadership role to him.

He took another sip of coffee as he eased down to sit on the steps. The cold weather was settling in. It was hard to believe Thanksgiving was next month. He'd gotten word that morning from his commanding officer that the team would be headed out again in late January. At least his teammates with families would get to spend the holidays with them. Gavin wondered if his grandmother would hang around the ranch this year. Because he was rarely home during the holidays, Gramma Mel usually flew to Saint Louis to spend time with her sister and her family.

"How did things go today with Caldwell and the men?"

Gavin glanced over his shoulder at the sound of his grandmother's voice. "Good, but that's no surprise. They know how to keep things going in my absence. And I covered just about everything with Phil yesterday. We talked again today and the books look good." The only thing he hadn't done that he'd wanted to do today was take another ride out to the dig site.

"When do you expect Mr. Clete back in town?" he asked.

"By the middle of next week," she said, taking a seat in the porch swing.

"Good." Although Gavin felt certain Clete was the one who'd moved the marker, he wanted to be absolutely sure. However, for the life of him, he couldn't imagine anyone else coming onto the property and tampering with Layla's markers. What purpose would it serve?

Flip's camera had picked up something underground, both in her marked spot as well as another spot close by. Like he'd told her, it was probably nothing more than bullet shells or branding irons. One section did have a relatively higher reading than others but he'd figured out a reason for that, as well. Buried Native American artifacts. Gavin's grandfather had claimed this had been Native American land generations ago. If Layla's research was as thorough as she claimed, she would already know that.

"I had a salad earlier, but if you're hungry I can fix dinner."

"No need. I plan to go into town in a few and I'll grab something at the café."

No way he would tell his grandmother that in addition to dinner he intended to make a booty call. Word was out that he was home and a ton of women had left voice mails. On the drive into town, he would decide which woman would be the recipient of his visit. Not having Layla was getting to him. He needed to get laid and then he could be more rational about her, take his time seducing her without losing his cool.

"Looks like you aren't the only one going into town, Gavin. Now, doesn't she look extra pretty?"

He followed his grandmother's gaze. Layla was crossing the yard and walking toward them. He had seen her in dresses before, but this was one with a skirt that was shorter in the front and longer in the back. Instead of boots she wore high heels and she had a knitted shawl around her shoulders.

Her hair was styled the way he liked best, flowing around her shoulders. And he could tell she was wearing makeup—not much…except for the ruby-red lip color. He frowned, refusing to let her get next to him the way she had last night. He'd been stupid enough to think their evening would end differently. Namely, in bed together.

"Good evening, Ms. Melody. Gavin."

He did the gentlemanly thing and stood. He couldn't help noticing she'd given his grandmother a huge smile. But the one she'd given him was forced. Not that it bothered him one iota.

"Layla," he said, letting his gaze roam all over her.

His grandmother moved forward and gave her a hug. "Now, don't you look pretty. Have big plans for the evening?"

Layla shrugged her shoulders, keeping her focus on Ms. Melody and ignoring Gavin. "Not that big. The equipment arrives tomorrow and my team the day after. Then it's all work and no play. I decided to spend my last day of freedom doing something I enjoy doing but rarely have time for—going to a movie."

"By yourself?" Gramma Mel asked.

Layla chuckled. "Yes, by myself."

"What are you going to see?"

"That new romantic comedy with Julia Roberts."

"Now, isn't that a coincidence. I was going into town to see that one myself," Gavin said.

Both Layla and Gramma Mel turned to stare at Gavin with raised brows. He smiled at both women's expressions. He then directed his next statement to Layla. "Since we're going to see the same movie, is there any reason we can't go together?"

Gavin was certain there was but he knew Layla wouldn't call him out on it in front of his grandmother. When she didn't say anything he leaned closer to ask, "Well, is there?"

As if recovering from her initial shock, she opened her mouth, probably to say something that would blister his ear. Then she quickly closed it, seeming to remember that his grandmother was standing there, listening to their exchange.

"No, there's no reason," she said. "I'm just surprised you would want to see a *chick flick*. I took you for a blood-and-guts sort of guy."

He shook his head. "As a SEAL, I see too much of that in real life. A chick flick should be interesting. Besides, I like Julia Roberts."

"In that case, I see no reason why we can't go together," she said.

Although she'd tried to sound cheerful about it, he knew she wasn't. Was that her teeth he heard grinding? "Great. We can go in my truck. I just need to grab my Stetson and jacket."

"I enjoyed the movie, didn't you?"

Layla had pretty much given him the silent treatment since leaving the Silver Spurs earlier but he didn't seem to mind. In fact he seemed amused by it. "Yes, I enjoyed it."

She probably would have enjoyed it even more had he not been there to cloud her concentration. It had been hard to focus on the huge movie screen with a sexy man sitting beside her.

"When are you going to stop acting childish, Layla?"

She glanced over at him. "Childish? You think *I'm* acting childish when you told me last night that we won't kiss again unless sex is part of the mix?"

"Yes, that's what I said and I meant it."

"Well, sorry if you think I'm acting childish

but I'm the one acting more adult than you. All you can think about is—"

"Making love to you."

She swallowed, seeing a picture of that very thing in her mind. "Yes."

"Can't help it. You do things to me, Layla."

When she was honest with herself, she could admit that he did things to her, as well. But she would never admit it to him. He was just like all the other men she'd known, which is why she'd sworn off relationships. All men wanted of a woman was a roll between the sheets. She wanted more from life; she had a career to build. Men and sex only got in the way of her goals.

She glanced over at him. "You were an only child, right?"

"Yes, as far as I know."

When she looked at him in surprise he added, "My mother deserted us when I was eight and never came back. For all I know, she could have married and had more kids by now."

Layla nodded. "She and your dad got a divorce?"

"No, but she might have changed her name and started over. Who knows?"

Layla didn't say anything for a moment. "You've never tried to find her?"

"No."

"Not even when your father was killed in the war?"

His jaw tightened. "Especially not then. If she didn't return to see him while he was living, I sure as hell didn't plan to give her the opportunity to see him dead," he said in a biting tone. "Dad always believed she would come back to us. Even said he understood her need to get away. After all, he'd talked her into coming to Cornerstone."

"Where was she from?"

"New York. Manhattan. They met while he was on military business at the United Nations. They'd only known each other a week when they married. They met one night at a restaurant, a month after her only family, an aunt, died."

"So when they met, she had no living family?"

"No."

He didn't say anything else for a long moment, and then he added, "According to Dad she lasted out here longer than he expected her to. She tried being a good wife, and I remember her being a good mom. Dad placed a lot of blame on himself since he had to carry out a lot of missions, leaving her here with Gramma Mel and Grampa Gavin. And when I came along a year later, he thought she'd adjusted."

"But she hadn't?"

"Evidently not. One day she up and left. She told my grandparents she needed to get away for a while and asked them to watch me. She said she'd be back before Dad returned from his overseas tour. Then she got in her car— the one Dad bought for her—and drove off."

"And she never came back?"

He shook his head. "No, she never came back. Months later, when Dad returned home and found her gone, he was heartbroken. She left him a note saying she would come back. But she never did."

"And after all this time, you've never tried finding her?"

"No. She decided she didn't want me or Dad in her life."

Gavin inwardly admitted that more than once he had thought about locating his mother, if for no other reason than to ask her why she never came back. One of his former SEAL teammates, Nick Stover, worked for Homeland Security. All Gavin had to do was give Nick her name and there was no doubt in his mind that Nick would tell Gavin her whereabouts. A part of him knew the main reason he hadn't done so was his fear of what he would find out. What if his mother had never wanted him or loved his dad? At times it was easier to do what his father had done and believe the best…even if it was a fairy tale.

He drew in a deep breath. Why had he shared any of that with Layla when he'd never shared it with a woman before? For some reason, when she'd asked if he was an only child, the floodgates had opened. Emotions he usually kept locked inside had come pouring out.

"Any other family besides Ms. Melody? What about aunts, uncles or cousins?"

He figured she was asking for conversational purposes only, so he obliged her. "My grandmother has a younger sister living in Saint Louis. Her only grandson, Benjamin, and I are close. We're more like brothers than cousins. He spent a lot of his summers here. Ben's a year older and in the Marines. Right now he's stationed in Afghanistan, and we're hoping he'll be home for the holidays."

He glanced over at her. "What about you? Any cousins?"

She shook her head. "No. My grandparents didn't have any siblings and they had one child. I never knew my mother's parents. They died in a boating accident when she was in her teens."

He said nothing as he drove. They were ten minutes from his home and although there had been sexual chemistry between them as usual, they'd managed to keep it under control. That was a surprise since his plans for this evening had originally been to end up in some woman's bed. A part of him couldn't believe he'd given up the chance for sex just to spend time in Layla's company. And he had to grudgingly admit that although she'd tried to ignore him for most of the evening, he had enjoyed being with her.

Moments later, he pulled into the yard in front of the ranch house. His grandmother would be leaving tomorrow and he would have the house all to himself. Bringing the car to a stop, he cut the ignition and turned to Layla. "I'll see you inside."

"That's not necessary," she said, already opening her door to get out. "Thanks for driving me
into town and joining me at the movies."

Although she'd said he didn't have to see her
in, he walked beside her anyway. "You're welcome, although I know you really didn't prefer
my company."

When she didn't deny what he'd said, he chuckled. "No wonder you don't have a boyfriend."

She glanced over at him. "What makes you
think I don't have a boyfriend?"

"I asked Gramma Mel if any man had visited
you here and she said no."

Layla frowned. "That doesn't mean anything."

He chuckled again. "Yes, it does. If you had a
boyfriend he would have come here, if for nothing else but to check on you. To see how you were
doing. To feel out the competition. To stake his
claim."

Even in the moonlight, he saw her roll her eyes.
"Not all men are territorial, Gavin."

"Any man connected to you would be."

They had made it to the porch. When he offered her hand to assist her up the steps, she said,
"No need." And then she walked up to the door

without his help. He knew why. All it would have taken was one touch and they would have lit up like the Fourth of July and they both knew it.

"Thanks for seeing me home. At least my temporary home."

"No problem. What time does the equipment arrive tomorrow?"

"Sometime before noon. Thanks again for allowing me to store the equipment in that old barn."

He nodded. "When will your team get here?"

"Some will start arriving the day after tomorrow and will be staying at a hotel in town. We're hoping to finish the dig in a couple of weeks and then we'll be on our way."

A couple of weeks. He had every intention of making love to her before she left. In the meantime, he planned to stick to his resolve about not kissing her until she was ready to give in to their desire—even if it killed him.

"Good night, Layla."

When she just stared at him, he smiled. Evidently she'd expected him to kiss her good-night. "I'll stand here until you go inside."

She nodded. "Good night." And then she quickly opened the door and went in.

He didn't move until he heard the lock click in place. Then he tilted his Stetson back from his face as he moved down the steps. Not kissing her had been hard but he meant what he'd told her yesterday. The next time they kissed would be when they made love. Just thinking about how intense that kiss would be sent heat through his body, especially to his lower extremities.

If he hadn't needed to meet with Caldwell and his men first thing in the morning, he would have taken another ten-mile run around the ranch.

Ten

Three days later, while out riding Acer, Gavin came upon Layla and her excavation team in the south pasture. Most of them had arrived a couple of days ago but he hadn't been around to meet them. He and his men had driven the cows to the north pasture where they would be kept during the winter months.

Over the next few weeks, the cows would be fed to maintain their good heath during the cold spell. Unlike the south pasture, there was plenty of grazing land in the north and a small pond to help irrigate the area. The pregnant cows had to be separated and tagged and the process had taken a lot longer than expected.

Just as well, he thought, as he brought Acer to a slow trot and then a complete stop at the top of the hill. He'd needed distance from Layla. With his grandmother in Cincinnati and him being out on the range for the past three days he'd assured their paths didn't cross.

But now he was back and as he looked down at the activity going on below, he couldn't stop his gaze from seeking her out. At first he didn't see her, but when the crowd dispersed somewhat, there she was, looking as beautiful as he knew she would be.

He rubbed his hand down his face. Nothing about this seduction was working out like he'd figured it would. It seemed he would be the one to break before Layla. He just didn't get it. They wanted each other. That was definite. So how could she keep fighting the attraction? Desire had to be eating away at her as much as it was at him.

He hadn't seen her since that night they'd gone to a movie. Seeing her now made him realize that after all those hot and steamy kisses, and copping one good feel of her thighs, she had gotten into his system. That was crazy. Women didn't get into his system—ever. So how had she managed it?

He fixed his gaze on her as if three days could have changed her. They hadn't. Even from where he sat unobserved on Acer's back, he could still see her flawless skin. She looked just as young as the members of her team. Her students. Wearing her hair in a ponytail, jeans, a pullover sweater and boots should have made her fit in. Yet there was something about Layla that stood out. Something that made his stomach churn and his groin ache every time he saw her.

He never did make it into town just for that booty call. The only woman he wanted was Layla.

Bottom line—she had stirred something deep inside of him that wouldn't go away. At least not until he was inside of her, all the way to the hilt. It was only when his body connected with hers that he would be able to rid his mind of the belief that she was the only woman for him.

Watching her team work, he remembered something else. Namely that phone conversation he'd had with Clete yesterday. The old man recalled seeing the marker. He'd known why it was there,

since he'd heard talk in town about someone digging on the property. But according to Clete, he
hadn't moved it. That made Gavin wonder who
had. Both he and Clete agreed the wind could
not have blown it away nor could it have gotten
washed away by the rain. Which meant someone had come on Gavin's property and pulled it
out. Why?

Gavin hadn't been receptive to the idea of Layla
digging on the Silver Spurs. But if someone was
intentionally setting her up to fail, they would
have to deal with him. Flip's camera had picked
up something buried here. That made Gavin wonder if someone intended to unearth whatever was
buried before Layla did so they could get the
credit? His jaw tightened at the thought. Not on
his property. And not on his watch. And not with
his woman.

His woman…

How in the hell could he consider her his
woman when he hadn't bedded her yet? Besides,
Gavin Blake never claimed any woman. But as
he fixed his gaze on Layla, he knew that she was
his. Bedded or not.

Layla had been reading what looked like a report when suddenly, as if she felt him watching her, she tilted her head up and stared straight at him.

A lump formed in Layla's throat. Beneath the brightness of the noon sun sat a gorgeous man on a beautiful horse. She'd seen the horse before. One day after arriving on the Silver Spurs, she'd noticed when one of the men had taken it out of the stall to groom it. She had been admiring the animal when the man, Curtis, told her the horse's name was Acer and that he belonged to the boss. This was the first time she'd seen Gavin on the horse and the sight took her breath away.

It had been three long days since he'd taken her to the movies and later walked her to the guest cottage, leaving her there and blatantly ignoring her since. Honestly, what had she expected? For him to have kissed her good-night regardless of what he'd said the night before? What he'd done was to toss the ball in her court. He probably figured she didn't have the guts to play it.

But it wasn't that she didn't have the guts. She didn't have the time or the inclination… Oh, who was she fooling? Definitely not herself. If anything, not seeing him these past few days had made her realize that out of sight, out of mind didn't work when it came to Gavin.

"Who in the blazes is that?"

Layla didn't have to move her gaze from Gavin to know one of her students, Tammy Clemons, stood beside her looking at Gavin, as well. "That's Gavin Blake. He and his grandmother own the Silver Spurs. They were kind enough to let us dig here."

"Um, maybe I should thank him. Properly."

A sudden stab of jealousy ran through Layla, and as much as she tried pushing it back, she couldn't. *Properly?* She didn't have to wonder just what Tammy meant by that. It was rumored around campus that Tammy often bragged about sleeping with her professors to get better grades.

Layla knew not to believe everything she heard, but Tammy's behavior made Layla think there was some truth in that claim. Especially since Tammy was here on this dig. Some said her latest conquest was Dr. Clayburn. That wouldn't surprise Layla since the married man and father of two was known to have roving eyes. More than once she'd heard about his late night meetings with female students. Those meetings were something Layla was certain the college president had heard about but had chosen to ignore.

Tammy's grades should have made her ineligible for this team, but Dr. Clayburn had personally added her name above other more well-deserving students. When Layla had brought it to Dr. Clayburn's attention, he'd gotten upset that she'd questioned him. He'd reminded her that he had the power to withdraw the school's funding for the excavation.

"That guy is what you would call a real cowboy. And I didn't have to travel to Texas to get one."

Layla saw the twenty-one-year-old lick her lips with her gaze trained on Gavin. It shouldn't matter to Layla. But it did. Why? She didn't want to be Gavin's bed partner so why should it bother her if someone else did?

"Need I remind you, Tammy, that you're here to work on this project?"

Tammy frowned. "No, Dr. Harris, you don't need to remind me of anything. Just like I'm sure I don't need to remind you that although we're dedicated to this dig during the day, the nighttime hours are ours to enjoy. And I intend to enjoy him."

The young woman stated the words so matter-of-factly that Layla had to take pause. Was Tammy the type of woman Gavin wanted? The kind who could handle both work and play without breaking a sweat? A woman who enjoyed the challenge of both?

Layla was about to reply when a huge smile covered Tammy's face. "He's seen me checking him out and is coming down for me."

The thought that Gavin might be showing some interest in Tammy made Layla's chest ache.

She turned her attention back to Gavin. He was sprinting down the hill on the huge horse and she recalled something he'd once said. When he saw a target he wanted he went after it. Was he now galloping down the hill because he wanted Tammy? The young woman evidently thought so.

He looked good on the horse, wearing a Stetson on his head. Tammy was right. He was the epitome of what a cowboy should be. Tough. Rugged. Fearless. But then she could probably use those same adjectives to describe him as a navy SEAL.

Gavin slowed his horse to a trot when it hit level ground and then he headed in their direction.

"Didn't I tell you he was coming to check me out?" Tammy said, with a ton of confidence in her voice.

The young woman didn't lack any faith in herself as a woman who could draw a man's interest. Gavin reached them and brought the horse to a stop. A lump formed in Layla's throat when she saw his attention hadn't even flickered to Tammy. He was staring straight at Layla.

"Gavin."

"Layla."

"And I'm Tammy," the younger woman quickly said, not waiting for an introduction. She flashed Gavin a huge, flirty smile.

Gavin switched his gaze from Layla to Tammy. "Hello, Tammy."

"You look good on your horse. I would love for you to give me a ride."

Gavin released a smooth chuckle. "Sorry. Acer is temperamental. I'm the only one he lets on his back."

"Um, I'm sure there are other ways we can

ride," Tammy purred suggestively. "Without your horse."

Layla cleared her throat. Did the young woman have no shame? Tammy had pretty much offered herself to Gavin. Talk about being over-the-top brazen. The smile, she noticed, didn't leave Gavin's features when he said, "Thanks. But no thanks." He then turned his full attention back to Layla. "Have dinner with me tonight."

Layla swallowed. "Dinner?"

"Yes. I figured we could grab a meal in town."

Before Layla could say whether she would go or not, Tammy spoke up in an irritated tone. "Dr. Harris is in charge of this project, and I'm sure she has a lot to do tonight since we start digging in a few days. There are preliminary reports she has to complete and soil samples that need to be reviewed. But I'll be glad to go out with you tonight."

An annoyed frown replaced the smile on Gavin's lips when he turned to Tammy. "Are you her spokesperson?"

It was obvious Tammy had been caught off guard by Gavin's question. "No."

"I didn't think so. As far as taking her place, I didn't ask you to, did I?"

He couldn't have been I'm-not-interested-in-you plainer than that, Layla thought. Rage appeared in Tammy's face, making it quite obvious she wasn't used to men rejecting her and she didn't appreciate Gavin doing so. Instead of answering his question, she turned and angrily strutted off.

Layla watched her go and then turned her attention back to Gavin. "You might have hurt her feelings."

He shrugged massive shoulders. "She'll get over it. Besides, someone needs to teach her some manners." He leaned back. "So what about it? Will you have dinner with me tonight? We can even take in another movie if you like?"

Layla nibbled at her bottom lip. Tammy had been right about her having a lot of work to do to prepare for the start of the dig. But then hadn't Tammy also reminded her that although they were dedicated to this dig during the day, the nighttime hours were theirs to enjoy? Besides, after witnessing Tammy come on to Gavin the way she had, Layla had realized something. He could have taken Tammy up on her bold offer but he hadn't. He had even made it crystal clear that Layla was the woman he wanted.

Though she had convinced herself that she could do without him even if she wanted him, she now knew she couldn't. And why should she? She'd spent her whole life proving she could accomplish what she set her mind to. Now, she was setting her mind to finishing this dig and having Gavin, too.

She had set her target and she was going after what she wanted. In other words, she was about to become Viper Jr.

She met Gavin's gaze. "Dinner and a movie sound nice. Yes, I'd love to go out with you tonight."

Eleven

The moment Layla walked up the porch steps her nerves tightened. Was she doing the right thing? Was following her desires rather than common sense the best move for her tonight?

Her gaze swept over at the man at her side. Gavin had been quiet since parking his truck. Now he was walking her to the door and she knew it would be her decision how tonight would end. He wouldn't even kiss her good-night unless he knew for certain more came with that kiss. Was she ready to give him more?

They had been careful not to touch all night. Holding hands would have led to heaven knows what. The sexual chemistry between them was that explosive. She had been aware of everything about him all evening. His breathing pattern, the sexual vibes that poured off him and the heavy-lidded eyes that stared at her.

Even now, there was this sensuous pull of desire between them. She was aware of it and she knew he had to be aware of it, as well. That consciousness was a slow roll of longing in her stomach and a throbbing intensity at the base of her throat. Never had she felt such primal awareness of a man before.

When they reached the door she turned to him. Although his Stetson shaded his eyes, she felt his stare. She inhaled his masculine scent. The man was a living, breathing sample of testosterone at its best.

Drawing in a deep breath, Layla tightened her hands on the shoulder straps of her purse. "Dinner was wonderful. So was the movie. It's been a long time since I've seen a musical." His taste in movies surprised her. Last time it had been a chick flick and tonight a musical.

"Glad you enjoyed both."

She smiled up at him. "I did. Thanks for asking me to go. To be with you."

He nodded. "I can't think of any other woman I'd rather have been with tonight, Layla."

His words sent profound happiness spiraling through her. He could have spent the evening with Tammy, who was almost six years younger, and to Layla's way of thinking, a lot prettier. But she was the one he'd asked out. "Thank you for saying that."

"It's the truth."

When she didn't respond, she heard Gavin draw in a deep breath before saying, "I know you have a lot of work to do so I'll let you get to it."

He was giving her an out. He wouldn't pressure her. He'd stated days ago where he stood. If things between them escalated it would be up to her.

Swallowing deeply, she asked, "Would you like to come in for a drink, Gavin?"

He held her gaze for a long moment before smiling. "Yes, that would be nice, Layla."

As she opened the door to let him in, Layla knew it would be a whole lot better than just nice.

Gavin followed Layla inside. Removing his Stetson, he placed it on the rack by the door.

She walked ahead, toward the living room and his groin tightened with each sinfully erotic sway of her hips.

"Beer or wine cooler?" she asked over her shoulder.

"Beer." He closed the front door. He actually needed something a lot stronger. A straight shot of bourbon might do the trick, to stop his testosterone from overloading. But then he figured there wasn't a drink on earth that could deaden his desire for Layla. It went too deep. He could actually feel a throb in his veins. Drawing in a deep breath he inhaled her scent.

"Here you are," she said, reentering the living room.

He recalled the last time she'd offered him a beer and what had occurred when their hands touched. What he'd felt. Would she avoid touching him this time? There was only one way to find out.

When she handed him the bottle, he deliberately held her gaze. Intentionally, he rubbed his finger against her hand. Hearing her sharp intake of breath, he'd gotten the reaction he'd hoped for.

Unlike the last time she didn't wipe her hands on her jeans.

Still holding her gaze, he opened the bottle and took a huge gulp. He then lowered the bottle, licked his lips and asked the same question he had asked that night. "Want a sip?"

He'd given her an opening. Instead of retreating like she had before, she covered the distance separating them. "Yes, I want a sip." But instead of taking it, she said, "I'd rather sip it from your lips."

He lifted the bottle to his mouth. Then she took the bottle from him and placed it on a nearby table before leaning up on tiptoes to place her mouth over his. With a boldness he hadn't expected from her, she wrapped her arms around his neck and began sipping the beer from his lips.

Gavin felt light-headed and hot at the same time. Never had a woman stirred such passion within him. Never had any woman made his erection throb to this point. Layla was full of surprises and she was driving him insane with need.

As their mouths mated, he wrapped his arms around her. He wasn't surprised by how fluidly her body aligned with his. Sensations swamped his body. He knew from the way she was tasting him that tonight would not end with this kiss. The mating of their mouths was just the beginning. Tonight they were on the same page.

He swept her into his arms. Breaking off the kiss, he whispered against her lips, "I'm taking you to bed, Layla. If you have a problem with it, you need to say so now."

A seductive smile touched her lips. "I don't have a problem with that, Gavin."

Sexual excitement rushed through his veins as he moved quickly toward the bedroom.

Twelve

When Gavin placed Layla on the bed she looked up at him and saw eyes filled with intense desire gazing down at her. She'd meant what she said about going to bed with him. But he might not feel the same way after she said what she had to say.

"We need to talk first, Gavin."

He pulled her sweater over her head. "Okay, I'm listening."

Was he really? Or was he concentrating on undressing her? "A while back you asked me when I last did this. Do you remember that conversation?"

Her sweater was off and his swift hands went to

the front clasp of her bra. Within seconds he had her breasts tumbling free. She watched his eyes get smoky as he stared at her nipples, which hardened as he watched. When he brushed against one with a feathery stroke of his fingertips, she drew in a sharp breath.

"Yes, I remember that conversation," he said in a husky voice, stroking her other breast as if fascinated with its size and shape. "What about it?"

Layla had to think a minute to remember the conversation. His hands were driving her insane. And when he began stroking her nipples in earnest, it created a throbbing ache in her center. She couldn't help but moan.

"Layla?"

"Um?"

"What about the conversation?"

What conversation? Her brain was turning to mush and she fought hard to recall what he was talking about. Then she remembered. "Are you ready for an answer to the question you asked?"

"Doesn't matter now."

And before she could draw in another breath, he lowered his head and eased a rigid nipple between his lips. He sucked hard, feasting in earnest. Greedily. Ravenously. At the same time, he eased the hem of her skirt toward her waist.

And then he pushed aside her panties to ease fingers inside of her. The moment she felt the intimate invasion, she shuddered in pleasure. How could his mere touch do that? Make her come so unglued? Make her feel like a woman?

And when those same fingers stroked her down there, with the same rhythm his tongue was using to suck on her nipples, she moaned aloud.

"That's it. Get all wet for me, baby. Your scent has been driving me mad for days now. I can't wait to taste you."

She wasn't sure what he meant. All she knew was Gavin Blake had fingers that should be considered illegal and a mouth that should be banned. Using both, and at the same time, should be forbidden.

Sensation gathered force in her stomach and when he sucked harder on her breasts, while at the same time inserting his fingers deeper inside of her, she could not bear the pleasure any longer. Her body began to shake with the need for release. A climax ripped through her body. On instinct, she threw her head back and screamed his name.

"Now for my taste."

Before she realized what Gavin was doing, he had pulled off her skirt and tossed it aside along with her panties. Before she could ask what he thought he was doing, he lifted her hips to his mouth and firmly settled his head between her legs.

Layla tried pushing him away—until the moment she felt his tongue ease between her womanly lips. He kissed her down there the same way he'd kissed her on the mouth. Deeply. Thoroughly.

She stopped pushing him away. Instead she grabbed his shoulders and held on. Held him. She needed him to stay right there and continue what he was so expertly doing. When she felt his tongue delve deeper inside, flicking back and forth, her body shattered into what felt like a million pieces.

"Gavin!"

He didn't let up. He continued using his mouth to drive her over the edge yet again. Never had she experienced anything so powerful. So utterly amazing. For a minute she thought she had passed out. Maybe she had. She was completely drained. Limp. Too weak to move. So she lay there, nearly convinced she had died and gone to heaven. Surely there was nothing on earth that could make her feel this good. This satisfied.

She didn't move. She couldn't find the strength to open her eyes. Not even when she heard him remove his clothes before he pulled her boots and socks from her feet. Not even when his hands stroked her thighs and eased them apart.

And not even when she heard the sound of a condom packet being ripped open.

Moments later she heard Gavin's deep voice directly above her. "Open your eyes, baby. Look at me."

Although her eyelids felt heavy, she somehow found the strength to force them open. Gavin's naked body was braced above hers and desire-filled eyes stared down at her. Was it her imagination or were his eyes getting even darker as she stared into them?

"I'm looking," she said softly. Not only was she looking but she was being held in some sort of hypnotic trance.

"I wanted you this way from the first moment I set eyes on you."

That was nice. And she was about to say something, she wasn't sure what, when she felt the hot tip of his erection press against the core of her womanhood.

Her gaze widened and she knew she needed to tell him. Now. "Gavin?"

He leaned in and kissed the words off her lips. Using that scandalizing tongue of his, he began driving her crazy. Instinctively her legs opened wider and she felt him pressing down gently, as he tried entering her body.

He broke off the kiss and stared down at her. She knew from his expression exactly when he realized the *something* she'd tried to tell him about. The *something* he'd said no longer mattered.

"You're a virgin," he whispered in shock.

"Yes." Would he change his mind? Would it matter? She swallowed and said quietly, "I'll understand if you no longer want me."

Something flickered in his dark gaze. "Why wouldn't I still want you? Because you're a twenty-six-year-old virgin?"

When she nodded, he smiled and said, "Doesn't bother me if it doesn't bother you."

That was the moment she knew she had fallen in love with Gavin. She had tried denying it, had even called herself several kinds of a fool for letting it happen. She'd never loved a man before, but she knew what her feelings were. For all the heartbreak it would cause when she left the ranch in a week or so, it didn't make much sense for her to love a man now. But her heart had declared Gavin was it and there was nothing she could do about it.

Making love with him seemed right in a way it had never been with any other man…which was the real reason why she had remained untouched all these years. Sex had never interested her. She had never been turned on by the mere thought of it. Things were different with Gavin. Even before she'd met him face-to-face, his pictures had done something to her. They had pretty much warned her of her fate but she'd refused to accept it until she'd welcomed him inside tonight.

"Layla?"

She held his gaze. "Doesn't bother me, either."

Please don't ask me why I chose you. At least not now.

He didn't ask her anything. Instead he kissed her before using his knee to widen her legs. And then she felt him, easing inside of her, inch by inch. He was big and she sucked in as he filled her deeply, her body stretching for his invasion. Her muscles clamped down—not to stop his journey but to make it even more sensuous for the two of them. He continued to ease deeper until there was no place left for him to go. He was fully embedded in her in a fit so snug and tight she couldn't tell where her body ended and his began.

When her muscles tightened even more, she actually felt his erection throb inside of her. "If you keep that up do you know what's going to happen?" He leaned in close to ask her.

"No."

"It's going to make me want to do this."

Then he began thrusting, gently, in a sensuous rhythm that drove her to lift her hips with his every downward stroke. When her inner muscles clenched him harder, he thrusted harder, with a steady fluid beat.

Too steady. Each stroke inside her body pushed

her to a place she'd never been. He'd made her come using his mouth. But this was different. It was more intense. Insanely gratifying. And when he went faster, harder, deeper, she screamed his name as sensations washed over her. She clawed at his back, bucked upward to tighten her legs around him and lock their bodies together.

An intense explosion swept her away in an earth-shattering release. Although this might be the first time she'd made love with a man, she knew that this wouldn't be her last with Gavin.

That had been totally unreal, Gavin thought, a short while later as he lay flat on his back staring up at the ceiling. When had making love to a woman ever left him so physically sated and mentally drained? Hell, he was used to making out with women, sometimes all night long. And as a SEAL he was physically fit for all the rigors of combat. Yet, the woman sleeping beside him had practically drained him, made him weak as water with their first sexual encounter. How was that possible?

And she'd been a virgin. Gavin didn't have to wonder how that was possible, given her status in life. To accomplish what she'd accomplished at her age meant she'd made sacrifices. He'd suspected her experience with men had been limited, he just hadn't figured it to be nonexistent. Not that it bothered him. Normally, he preferred not to be any woman's first, but he was glad he'd been Layla's. The thought that no other man had been inside her body before him felt good, made him want to beat on his damn chest like a caveman. He'd branded Layla as his.

His?

Where in the hell had that thought come from? This was the second time he'd thought of her as being his woman. His. He needed to remind himself once again that he wasn't into possessiveness. He'd even participated in a ménage à trois a time or two during his college years. So the idea of laying claim to any woman didn't sit well with him. Sex was sex, no matter how good it was. No need to act crazy.

So why was he?

As he tilted his head to stare down at the woman sleeping peacefully beside him, he had to admit the sex had been better than good. Off the charts. He had studied her face when she'd come. Her expression had been utterly and incredibly spellbinding. Beautiful. Touching. She was such a passionate being it was hard to believe she'd held out for this long. Her presence on the Silver Spurs was the best luck he'd had in years. With sex that good she could dig up the entire damn ranch looking for whatever treasure she wanted. His treasure was right here with him in this bed.

Gavin frowned. He was thinking like a lovestruck puppy, and he refused to go there. Isn't that what had happened to his father? He'd quickly fallen in love with a woman only to die of a broken heart in the end? Okay, it had been an enemy's bullet that had taken him out, but Gavin of all people knew of his father's heartache.

Layla shifted her weight. Her leg, which rested between his, touched his groin. Immediately, he got hard. His erection had no problem coming to life. He glanced over at the clock. It was almost two in the morning. He should leave but the thought of waking up beside her in the morning had an appeal he couldn't dismiss.

And then there was the temptation to wake her now and make love to her all over again. Move between her legs and slide inside of her. Go deep until he couldn't go anymore. Then he would thrust hard like he'd done before. Even harder since she was no longer a virgin. He even thought about how it would feel not to wear a condom. To blast off inside of her. Fill her with the very essence of him.

Now that was taking his imagination a little too far. He was a man who played it safe so he would never be sorry. Babies of any kind were not in his immediate future. So why did the thought of a daughter who would be a mini-Layla appeal to him? Make his erection even harder?

Gavin closed his eyes. He had to stop thinking with the wrong head. Doing so could get him in serious trouble. He couldn't let sexual feelings take control of his common sense no matter how wrapped up he wanted to get with the woman beside him. No matter how much inhaling her arousing scent was getting to him.

Shifting his body, he pulled Layla closer and let sleep overtake him.

Thirteen

The strong aroma of coffee woke Layla. She blinked, and then sluggishly realized where she was and what she'd done last night and with whom. If there had been any doubt in her mind about what had happened, all she had to do was tilt her head to gaze across the room to where a half-naked man lounged in the doorway holding a steaming cup of coffee.

Gavin.

She blinked. Okay, since he was wearing jeans, he wasn't half-naked but half-dressed. Still, that was all he was wearing. And those jeans were riding low on his hips, making it pretty obvious just what a well-built body he had. His pose was picture perfect. He was the epitome of a sexy cowboy. A wealthy rancher. A scrumptious navy SEAL. How could one man exemplify all three and do it so well?

Her gaze roamed over him, from the top of his head all the way down to his bare feet. She'd paused when she'd seen that his zipper was undone. He'd either dressed quickly and hadn't bothered to zip up, or he had plans that included her so he'd figured why bother.

Those tantalizing thoughts made her recall last night. Her first time. And she knew without a doubt it had been worth the wait. She couldn't help it. Her gaze traveled the full length of him all over again. This time when her gaze settled on his midsection, she saw something she hadn't seen before. A huge erection. She drew in a deep breath and swore that it got bigger as she stared at it.

"Want some?"

She snatched her gaze from his groin up to his face. The smile that touched his lips was priceless and way too sexy for words. "What are you offering?" she asked.

"Whatever you want."

Reluctantly, she broke eye contact with him to glance outside the bedroom window. It was still dark but she knew it would be daybreak soon. Her team would be arriving from town within an hour or so. Her gaze returned to his. "I should take the coffee, get up, shower and get dressed."

"But..."

How had he known there was a *but* in there? "But I much prefer taking the man holding the coffee."

His smile widened. "And the man holding the coffee doesn't have a problem with you taking him."

Layla was only beginning to fully understand what heated lust was all about. "Did I tell you that last night I thought of myself as Viper Jr?"

He lifted a brow. "Viper Jr?"

"Yes. I set my sights on my target and went after what I wanted, and you, Gavin Blake, were my target."

A wry grin split his lips. "Was I?"

She nodded. "I wanted you."

"And I wanted you."

Layla then saw a somewhat serious look appear in his eyes as he said, "How do you feel?

I wanted you so much…because of that you're probably sore. You sure you're up to another ride this soon?"

Ride? She inwardly chuckled. Yes, he'd definitely ridden her last night. And yes, she was sore from it. However, as far as she was concerned, he could ride the soreness away.

"I'm sure."

"In that case." Placing the coffee cup on a nearby table, he crossed the room to the bed. "But first I want to see something." Before she could blink, he threw the bedcovers aside to expose her naked body.

Surprised, she scrambled to get back under the covers but he tossed them aside again. "No. Don't cover yourself. I just had to make sure I hadn't imagined anything. That you were as beautiful and delectable as I remembered. My mind didn't play tricks on me last night."

His words touched her. Made her feel wonderful. Made her feel like a real woman who had sexual feminine powers over a man. And when she watched him lick his lips with the tip of his tongue, she couldn't help remembering just where that tongue had been and what it had done.

Recalling that part of their lovemaking sparked an ache between her legs. As if he knew what sensations were enthralling her and where, he slowly eased his jeans down his strong, muscular thighs. Just as she'd thought. The jeans were the only thing he'd been wearing. He hadn't bothered to put back on his briefs.

"Now for this."

His words grabbed her attention and she watched him slide a condom over his erection. And boy was it large. How had it gotten inside of her last night? But he'd managed it and she knew he would again. This was the first time she'd seen a man prepare himself for sex. From the way he was doing it, it was obvious he was used to doing it.

"Ready?"

"Yes." She drew in a deep breath. The ache between her legs had made her nipples harden like tight buds.

"We're going to try something different this morning. It will be easier on you and help with your soreness."

In a way, she felt embarrassed engaging in such a conversation with him…about her body. But she

pushed her discomfort aside. After last night—
and all he'd done to her and how he'd done it—
there was no room left for shame. "What?"

He smiled as he moved back toward the bed.
"I want you to ride me."

She swallowed. "Ride you?"

"Yes. Do you know how to ride?"

She nodded. "Yes. My parents own several
horses." And she'd ridden them often enough.

"Good. So show me what you know," he said,
lying back on the bed beside her, then lifting her
over him. Just like that. As if she was weightless.

"I'll do my best," she said, sliding into position. The long, hard length of his erection was
like a rod, standing straight up, ready for her to
mount. So she did. Widening her legs, she took
him into her body. The hot texture of his male
organ seemed to blaze her insides as she took
him fully inside of her.

She watched his face, the same way she'd
known he'd watched hers last night. Their gazes
held. No words were spoken. This was all about
feeling. And she felt him in each and every part
of her body. Her muscles clenched around him.

Holding tight. And then as if of one accord they shivered with a need they both felt.

"Okay Viper Jr. Ride me, baby. Hard."

Gavin's words incited her to move up and down. She felt him grip the sides of her hips— to hold on to her, to guide her. Then, as if something elemental had taken control, she threw her head back and rode him hard.

What was happening to her? It was as if she'd lost control of her mind and her body. Having sex with Gavin this way, with her on top, riding him, sent an exhilarated feeling through her, one she couldn't explain.

When he leaned up and whispered naughty words in her ear, sinfully erotic words, she went mad with lust. She heard the bedsprings as she continued to ride. Each time her body came down against him, his came up to meet her.

Suddenly her quivering became uncontrollable and she felt her body explode into a thousand pieces. It was then that Gavin caught the back of her head with his hands and brought her mouth down to his, kissing her with a hunger that made her climax all over again.

Once again he came with her. She felt it. As

their tongues continued to mingle, she knew that she loved him with a passion she would never rid herself of, no matter the distance between them. While she was here on the Silver Spurs, she intended to make memories that would last her long after she returned to Seattle.

"Well, how did your dinner date with the handsome rancher go? Did the two of you do the nasty, Dr. Harris?"

Layla didn't immediately look up from studying the soil samples. Tammy was the last person she wanted to talk to, but to ignore her student would be rude. Yet no student had the right to inquire how their professor spent their evening. Layla had always maintained a distance between herself and her students. Because of her age, she took pains to ensure they never lost sight of the fact that she was their professor. As far as she was concerned, Tammy's question was out of line and lacked respect.

Layla raised her head from the microscope and met Tammy's gaze. "I don't think that should be your concern, Tammy. Did you finish your report?" Layla knew she hadn't. Several students had brought it to her attention that Tammy was slacking. It seemed whenever there was hard work to do, Tammy had a tendency to disappear.

Tammy scrunched up her features. "No. And why do I have to be the one to do that report? Donnell has a lot of free time."

"Only because Donnell has finished all his assignments. You haven't."

A smile touched Tammy's lips. "Doesn't matter. I'll still ace this class."

Layla frowned. "Not if you don't do your share of the work. And if you're not going to be a team player, I will have to replace you. There are several students who would love to be here."

"Doesn't matter. They don't have the connections I have," Tammy bragged. "I'm on this team, Dr. Harris, whether you want me here or not. I thought you understood that."

Layla refused to get into a confrontation with a student. It was clear Tammy thought that being Dr. Clayburn's occasional bed partner meant she could do whatever she wanted. Wrong. Not on Layla's team. "The only thing I understand is that I expect you to carry your load. If you can't, then you're out of here."

Tammy tossed her hair as a smirk touched her lips. "Wrong. You'll be out of here before I will. I'll make sure Mark…I mean Dr. Clayburn knows I'm being harassed." She then turned and sulked as she walked out the door.

In frustration Layla rubbed her hand down her face. Tammy might be right. Layla wasn't one of Dr. Clayburn's favorite people and it was obvious the man was quite taken with Tammy. And Tammy knew it.

"She'll eventually hang herself and Dr. Clayburn. Don't waste your time worrying about her, Dr. Harris."

Layla turned to find another one of her students, Donnell McGuire, standing in the doorway. Had he overheard her conversation with Tammy? Did he and the other students suspect something was going on between Tammy and Dr. Clayburn? The one thing Layla wouldn't do was discuss one student with another, no matter how much she wanted to sound off to someone about Tammy's atrocious attitude.

Before she could say anything, Donnell added, "And don't worry about that report Tammy hasn't done. I'll take care of it. I do have some free time."

His words told Layla he *had* overheard her conversation with Tammy. "That assignment was given to Tammy, Donnell, and I expect her to do it. Besides, I have something else for you to do. I just got a call that the last of our supplies arrived at the post office in town. I need you to go pick them up. If everything looks good, we'll start digging by the end of the week."

A huge smile touched Donnell's face. "Alright! I can't wait." The young man rushed off to tell the others.

Layla chuckled at his enthusiasm. She would give anything for more students like Donnell who took being a team player seriously. He was a hard worker. Most of the students on this team were. Although being an archaeologist was Donnell's first love, she knew he was also good with a camera and had won a number of photo contests. At twenty-two he would be graduating in the spring with a major in archaeology and a minor in photography.

She refused to let Tammy put a damper on her day, especially when it had started off with the promise of being wonderful. She'd had such a wonderful night with Gavin. Then this morning, before the crack of dawn, she'd proven just what a great horsewoman she could be. Memories of what they'd shared still sent shivers down her spine. She couldn't help but blush. Being intimate with a man had never been anything she'd thought about until now…

She glanced at her watch. She had a full day planned here on-site and then Gavin had invited her to dinner again. This time he would be the one cooking. He claimed he wasn't bad in the kitchen. Tonight she intended to see if that was true.

Gavin had always prided himself on being a man in control. As a SEAL, he couldn't be any other way. The success of any mission called for it. There was no time to let your guard down. Weakness of any kind wasn't acceptable. Then why did he lose control every time he entered Layla's body? Why did overpowering weakness overtake him whenever they made love?

He had prepared dinner for her tonight at the party house. He'd fed her well. Surprised the hell out of her with his culinary skills. At the moment, he contemplated impressing her with another skill. One of seduction. When he'd arrived at the party house with his arms filled with groceries, Layla had opened the door wearing an outfit that only made him think of filling her.

She'd tempted him the entire time he was in the kitchen. There was no doubt in his mind that she'd known exactly what she was doing as she'd sat at the breakfast bar watching him. She had known each and every time she crossed and uncrossed her legs that she was showing him a portion of her thigh and exactly what that did to him. How he had managed to finish cooking and then sit across from her and eat was a testament to his control.

Now it was payback time.

"So how was your day, Gavin?"

He'd cleared off the table and was loading up the dishwasher as he fought to retain control. "It was the usual day in the life of a rancher. The cows are finally settled in for the winter, which is good since forecasters predict a cold wave coming through first of next week."

"I heard. I'm hoping bad weather won't delay the completion of the dig. Our goal is to start later this week."

He closed the dishwasher door, then turned around and watched her gaze shift from his face to his midsection. She saw the evidence of his desire for her. That couldn't be helped when she was sitting there looking as sexy as any woman had a right to look. "Did I tell you how much I like your outfit?"

She chuckled and the sound made his erection thicken even more. "Yes, you told me. I figured you would like it since I understand men like to see skin."

She understood right. Men liked touching and tasting skin as well, which was something he'd shown her last night. Her short dress showed a lot of her thighs since the hem barely covered them. And the top had a neckline that showed a lot of cleavage, reminding him of how much he enjoyed her breasts. He wanted her bad. He wanted her right here. Right now.

He slowly crossed the room toward her. Any other woman would have run after seeing the predatory look in his eyes. But Layla stood her ground. That was fine with him. When he reached her, he removed her dress with a flick of his wrist and a little muscle power, leaving her totally naked. Like he'd suspected, she hadn't had a stitch of clothing on underneath that dress. He knew he had surprised the hell out of her with how quickly he'd undressed her.

He smiled at her shocked look. "A SEAL pays attention to detail. While sitting across from you at dinner I studied the design of your dress and figured out the best way to take it off without ripping it to shreds. I like the dress too much to tear it."

He stepped back. "Now to remove my clothes."

Gavin undressed quickly. And then he picked her up and spread her across the same table he'd cleared just moments ago. "Open your legs for me, Layla."

He intended to bury himself inside of her as deeply as he could go. He was certain the hot and hungry look in his eyes said as much. But he knew all this was still new to her and he wanted her to be comfortable with everything they did together.

She lay there, on his table, with her legs spread. For a minute he just stood and looked at her. Remembering her taste, he couldn't help but lick his lips. Tasting her would have to come later. Right now he needed to *come*. Quickly putting on a condom, he settled his body between her thighs. She held his gaze when he entered her, filling her completely. Being inside her, feeling her muscles clench around him, felt so damn good. Her muscles were trying to pull everything out of him and the sensation was driving him insane.

Gavin held tight to her hips as he moved in and out. She wrapped her legs around his waist, locking him inside of her. He wanted her to feel every stroke, the same way he was feeling it. On and on, each thrust was hard and precise. Back and forth, he rocked inside of her. Steady, with meaningful precision. He thrust hard, creating pleasure that spread like molten heat throughout both of their bodies. The sound of Layla's moans only increased his desire to please her. When he felt her body explode, his explosion soon followed.

That's when he realized why things were so

different with her. Why with her he so easily lost control.

As much as a part of him wished it wasn't true, he knew he had fallen head over heels in love with Layla Harris.

Fourteen

"So what are you going to do about Tammy?"

Layla lifted her head off Gavin's chest. It was two days after the night he'd prepared dinner for her. She had arrived at the guest cottage to find him sitting on the steps waiting for her. Her heart had pounded the minute she'd seen him sitting there. He'd stood when she got out of the car and her gaze had taken him in. With the Stetson on his head, his Western shirt, a pair of well-worn and scuffed boots, he looked like a quintessential cowboy. She wondered how he would look dressed as a SEAL. Too bad she would probably never see him that way. Gavin as a rancher would be the memory of him she would keep in her heart forever.

He had taken her hand into his and once they were locked inside the house, he had swept her into his arms and headed for the bedroom where they'd made love a number of times. Then he'd told her some troubling news. It seemed earlier that day he'd overheard one of his men bragging about sleeping with Tammy. The man had said she'd told him she was into group sex, so if he had any friends who were interested, she was available.

Gavin hadn't liked what he'd overheard and felt he needed to bring it to Layla's attention. She was glad he had. Unfortunately, she was battling her own issues with Tammy. The young woman's promiscuity wasn't Layla's number one concern. Tammy's entitled attitude was impairing the success of the dig. The report Layla had assigned to Tammy had yet to be done, and Tammy's slacking off on her duties had increased to the point where the other students were complaining. Low morale was the last thing Layla needed to deal with.

Layla had confided in Gavin, telling him of her

own issues with Tammy including Tammy's on-going affair with the head of Layla's department and how Tammy was blatantly using that affair to do whatever she wanted…as well as avoiding the things she didn't want to do.

Finally answering Gavin's question, Layla said, "There's only one thing I can do about Tammy and that is to release her from the team and brace myself for the backlash from Dr. Clayburn. She isn't a team player, she lacks respect for everyone and she isn't pulling her own weight. I refuse to give her more chances than I would give anyone else, no matter who she's sleeping with."

Gavin nodded. He thought Layla was making the right decision by releasing Tammy from her team. He'd known Tammy had been trouble from day one. "So you'll start digging on Friday?"

"Yes. We got delayed when one of the supply shipments was late. We haven't had any other problems, but I wanted to ask, did you ever talk to that guy to see if he was the one who moved my marker?"

"Yes, and Clete said he didn't move anything. So what happened to your marker is still a mystery."

"It doesn't matter since we're moving ahead. I'm excited."

He pulled her tighter into his arms. "So am I. I can't wait to see what you find."

She pulled back and stared up at him. "And now you think I will find something?"

"Yes. I told you I'd gotten a good reading from Flip's camera. I'm sure you'll find something, I'm just not certain it's the loot you're looking for."

She smiled up at him. "Well, I am certain, Mr. Blake." She then pulled his mouth down to hers.

Hours later, the ringing of his cell phone woke Gavin. He looked down at the woman plastered to his side. The phone had awakened her, as well. He glanced at the clock and saw it was three in the morning. Who would be calling him at this hour?

He reached for the phone on the nightstand before it could ring again. "Hello."

He heard the words his foreman said and was out of bed in a flash. "We're on our way."

Layla sat up. "What's wrong, Gavin?"

He glanced over at her as he reached for his clothes. "That was Caldwell. The old barn is going up in flames."

It didn't take long for them to both make their way to the south pasture.

"Arson?" Gavin asked, staring down Cornerstone's fire marshal. He knew Josh Timbales well since the man had been good friends with Gavin's dad.

"Yes, Gavin. Arson. And the person didn't even try covering their tracks. You could smell kerosene a mile away."

"But who would do such a thing?" Layla asked, staring at the building that was now burned to the ground as well as the charred remains of the equipment that had been stored inside.

"I don't know," Josh said to Layla. "My investigative team has been called in as well as the sheriff. Hopefully they will come up with some answers."

In the meantime... Layla turned to stare at her students who were huddled together a few feet away. They'd gotten word about the fire and had rushed from town. She could see the disappointed looks on their faces. They'd worked hard and now this. "I need to talk to my team," Layla said, and walked off.

Gavin watched her go. He could feel her anger and disappointment. He turned a livid gaze to Josh. "No matter what it takes, I intend to find the person responsible for this."

Layla approached the group. Before she could say anything, one of her students, Wendy Miller, spoke up. "Is it true what the firemen are saying? Did someone deliberately set fire to the barn?"

Layla drew in a deep breath. "Yes, the fire marshal has ruled it as arson. The sheriff is on his way."

"Looks like you have an enemy, Dr. Harris," Tammy said with a smirk. "Well, with no equipment for the dig, that means we're free to leave and return home, right? I didn't like this place anyway."

Layla had had enough. "Yes, you can leave, Tammy. I was going to release you from the team in the morning anyway. Have a safe trip back to Seattle."

Fury shone on Tammy's face. "You're dropping me from the team? You can't do that."

"I just did."

Tammy lifted her chin. "It really doesn't matter because there won't be a dig team. Once Dr. Clayburn calculates the cost of all the equipment that was destroyed in the fire, he will call off the dig."

"The college probably insured the equipment. It won't take long to get more in here," Donnell said angrily. He stared at Tammy suspiciously. "And just where were you tonight, Tammy? I was in the hotel's lobby and saw when you came in rather late. It wouldn't surprise me if you torched this place."

From the looks on the faces of her other students, Layla could see they were thinking the same thing. Evidently Tammy saw it, as well. She backed up, away from the others. "I was with someone, so I have a concrete alibi. But I plan on giving Dr. Clayburn a call to tell him everything."

"And how do you have his phone number?" another student asked, making it pretty obvious all of them had an idea.

"That's none of your business," Tammy snapped. And then she angrily walked off.

Layla turned back to her students. "I will call Dr. Clayburn in the morning myself. Regardless of what Tammy says, I doubt he will shut down the project."

Although Layla said the words, she truly wasn't so sure of that.

The next day, an angry Layla slammed down the phone. She could not believe the conversation she'd just had with Dr. Clayburn. She could not believe the audacity of the man.

"What's wrong, Layla?"

She turned and saw Gavin. She hadn't heard him enter the cottage. She saw the care and concern in his expression and she loved him even more than she already had. He had been so understanding and supportive. Incredibly, he'd been more concerned about the loss of her equipment than he had for the loss of his barn.

Last night they had both talked to the sheriff, whom she'd discovered was a high school friend of Gavin's. Sheriff Roy Wade was just as determined as Gavin to find the person responsible for the fire. And after checking for footprints, Gavin mentioned the ones around the burned barn were the same ones he'd seen when her marker had gone missing. It was obvious someone was trying to sabotage the dig. But who, and why?

She drew in a deep breath. "That was Dr. Clayburn."

"And?"

She blew out a frustrated and angry sigh. "Tammy got to him first. She probably called him last night like she threatened to do. He really didn't want to hear anything I had to say."

Gavin crossed his arms over his chest with a furious look on his face. "You mean to tell me he's taking a student's word over yours?"

Layla frowned. "Remember Tammy isn't just another student. She's also the man's side piece. I didn't want to believe it before, but I definitely believe it now. The influence she has over him! If I didn't know better I'd think there's more to it, that she's blackmailing him with something."

Gavin dropped his arms and came to stand in front of her. "Why? What did he say?"

"He wanted to let me know my students were notified this morning by email that the dig has been canceled and they are to return to campus." She paused. "He also wanted me to know that I've been terminated from my position at the university."

"He fired you?"

"Yes. He claims I botched things up. As far as he is concerned, the fire was my responsibility. I should have been more attentive to my work rather than indulging in an 'illicit affair with one of the cowboys.'" There was no doubt in Layla's mind Tammy had fed the man that BS and he'd believed it without question.

"Can't you go to the president of the university with your side of the story?"

"Yes, but Dr. Clayburn and President Connors are good friends. If I was terminated that means Dr. Connors approved the termination because he believed whatever Dr. Clayburn told him about me."

"Let them believe whatever they want. You came here to do a dig and that's what you'll do."

Layla dropped into a nearby wingback chair. "Gavin, didn't you hear what I said?"

He squatted down in front of her. "What I hear

is the sound of you giving up. Letting them defeat you."

She touched his cheek. "What am I supposed to do? I don't have a job. Nor do I have a team. Did you not hear me say that Dr. Clayburn sent everyone an email telling them to return to Seattle?"

"You'll get another job. You're too smart and intelligent not to. As far as I'm concerned, losing you is the university's loss. Besides, I want to see what their reaction will be when you find James's loot. You don't have to be affiliated with any university to dig or publish your findings, right?"

Layla shook her head. "No, I can conduct an independent excavation, but I no longer have funding, or a team."

Gavin pulled her out of the chair. "I'll replace your equipment. And you might not have a team, but I do. They will come to help out if I call them."

Layla stared at him, not believing what he was saying, what he was offering. "B-but I can't let you do that. Like you, they just got back from their last operation. They need to spend time with their families and—"

Gavin lowered his mouth and kissed the words

off her lips. He then deepened the kiss. By the time he released her mouth, she was panting. "Trust me on this, will you?" he said. "I don't want to brag or anything, but we will do it in half the time your team would have."

"But it will take time to get more equipment."

"We will get the equipment we need without any delays."

Layla knew he had money and influence. She just hadn't realized how much. Then she thought of something crucial. "What about the person sabotaging the dig? Things could get dangerous."

A sinister grin touched Gavin's lips. "If he or she is crazy enough to try something with a team of SEALs around, then let them go for it. We will be ready."

He quickly kissed her again, silencing any more questions. When he released her lips, he said, "Trust me. We've got this. We'll have your back."

There was a knock at the door. Gavin lifted a brow. "Gramma Mel isn't due back until tonight, so it might be Roy. Maybe he's found something."

Gavin crossed the room with her following beside him. Opening the door they found three of her students standing there. "Donnell? Wendy?

Marsha? What are you doing here?" Layla asked them. "Why aren't you on your way back to Seattle? Didn't you get Dr. Clayburn's email?"

"Yes, we got it," Donnell said, frowning. "But we didn't want to leave until we talked to you. Until you say there won't be a dig, we are staying put."

"You could get into trouble if you defy Dr. Clayburn," she warned them.

The three students looked at each other and shared what looked like conspiratorial smiles before Donnell said, "We aren't worried about that. They'll be faced with their own troubles soon. So, are you still planning to dig?"

Layla wondered what they meant by "troubles," but before she could ask, Gavin said, "Yes, the dig is still on."

She could tell from the look of respect in his eyes that he admired the stance these three students had taken. Like his team had his back, these members of her team had hers.

Donnell, Marsha and Wendy let out loud cheers and gave each other high fives. Then Donnell said, "When we find James's loot, the university's going to regret letting you go."

Fifteen

"So…you're the fast-talking college professor, huh?"

Layla swallowed as she watched the four men standing in front of her. Gavin had introduced them as Flipper, Bane, Coop and Mac. It was Flipper who'd asked the question, the depths of his blue eyes dancing with amusement.

All four were big men. Muscular. Well built. Extremely handsome. Two wore wedding rings and two did not. Gavin had told her that Brisbane Westmoreland and Thurston McRoy were happily married and that Flipper and Coop were happily single.

"I don't know. Am I?" she asked, switching

her gaze from them to Gavin, who stood by her side with his arms around her waist. It was as if he was intentionally making a statement regarding the nature of their relationship. If that was the case, then she wished someone would tell her where they stood. All she knew for certain was that they enjoyed spending time together and they shared a bed every night. She definitely didn't have any complaints about that.

Gavin muttered the words, "Smart-ass," to Flipper, then leaned down and placed a kiss on Layla's lips. He then turned to his friends. "She's more than a professor."

He knew his friends were checking out Layla and with good reason. The four men knew about his don't-get-attached policy when it came to women. But it was obvious that with this particular woman, he'd gotten attached. They would be shocked to discover just how attached he was.

Like he'd known they would, his friends had answered his summons for help. No questions asked. But now that they were here and had been briefed on the situation, they were also eyewitnesses to his possessiveness of Layla.

They would have questions about that later. Fair enough. He would address them then. He would admit he'd fallen in love. Bane and Mac would understand. Flipper and Coop would suggest Gavin have his head examined.

"Did you get the equipment I asked you to bring?" he asked them.

"Yes. Two of my brothers will be towing the backhoe loader and tractor in this evening," Flipper said.

"And I've got the rest of the stuff in my truck," Mac added.

"Good," Gavin said. Flip had four brothers. All SEALs. And Flip's dad had retired as a SEAL commanding officer. Gavin had thought he'd had it bad living in his father's and grandfather's shadows—until he'd met Flipper. His friend had five legacies to compete with since all the male Holloways before Flip had stellar reputations as SEALs.

"So where are we staying, Viper? The party house?" Coop asked.

Gavin shook his head. "No. Layla's at the party house."

Flipper chuckled. "So? It's big enough. You don't mind if we crash, do you?" he asked Layla.

Before she could answer, Gavin said, "But I mind."

All four men laughed. Gavin scowled.

"Easy, Viper, let's not get territorial," Flipper said, grinning.

But he did feel territorial, Gavin thought. He figured it was all a part of being in love. He still wasn't sure what to do with his feelings. He didn't want to get caught up in a woman like his dad had done. He didn't want to ask her to give up her career to wait out here on the ranch through all his missions. He didn't want a repeat of what had happened with his mom.

Pushing all that aside, he said, "Gramma Mel got back from her trip a few days ago and she prepared rooms for you guys at the main house."

"Yes!" Bane said, pumping his fist in the air. "We'll get to eat her mouthwatering biscuits for breakfast."

Gavin shook his head. He had to admit he'd missed these guys.

* * *

"So, are you going to tell Layla how you feel about her, Viper?"

Instead of answering Bane's question Gavin stared into his beer bottle and shook his head. "Won't do any good. She doesn't feel the same way."

"How do you know?" Mac asked, taking a sip of his own beer. "Women like to hear stuff like that. And often."

Coop and Flipper, Gavin noticed, were keeping their mouths shut. His admission that he'd fallen in love had shocked them into silence. The five of them were sprawled in the living room of the party house. Layla was at the main house assisting Gramma Mel with dinner. Gavin figured his grandmother would go all out and prepare a feast. She'd been happy to see his friends and they'd been happy to see her. Of course Bane would be getting those biscuits for breakfast in the morning. Mac had put in his order for an apple pie and both Coop and Flipper requested peach cobbler.

"So who do you think is trying to sabotage the dig?" Flipper asked, obviously trying to change the subject to one he and Coop could take part in. Gavin was glad to leave the topic of his love life behind.

"Don't have a clue but I intend to find out," Gavin said. "I thought it was someone connected to the university, but now I'm not sure."

"Sounds like someone doesn't want anyone digging in the south pasture, Viper," Coop said, standing, stretching out his limbs. "You all know I'm a suspicious bastard by nature. I can smell a cover-up a mile away."

Mac leaned forward in his chair. "You think someone is covering up something?"

"Possibly," Coop said. He glanced over at Gavin. "Other than Caldwell, how well do you know the men who work for you?"

Gavin shrugged. "Most have worked here for years, some even during my dad's time. There are two new guys we brought on last year." He recalled both were single, and he specifically remembered that one of them had shared Tammy's bed.

"What if someone knows for certain the loot is buried around here, heard about the dig and doesn't want anyone else to find it before they do?" Flipper suggested.

Gavin nodded. That possibility had crossed his mind, as well. He knew these four men. In addition to helping with the dig, they intended to solve the mystery of who'd removed the marker and burned down the barn. So far, the sheriff hadn't found anything other than those footprints. Gavin had mentioned the prints to his friends. "Um, that gives us something to go on," Mac said pensively.

"We start digging in the morning," Gavin said, leaning back in his chair. "Whoever doesn't want us to will either try to stop us or will hope whatever they don't want us to find is kept hidden."

Later that night, after making love to Layla, Gavin pulled her tighter into his arms as he tried to bring his breathing under control. She had ridden him again. She was getting too good at it. He was convinced the woman was trying to kill him.

"I like your friends, Gavin."

He decided not to tell her that they liked her, as well. They had joked with her at dinner and Bane had even told her about his wife, Crystal, who, like Layla, had gotten her PhD at an early age.

"I'm glad you like them."

Dinner had been a grand affair. Not only had his grandmother cooked enough food for his friends and Layla's students, she'd invited Caldwell and his men to stop by for a plate. Several of their neighbors who'd heard about the fire stopped by to make sure all was well. Gramma Mel had sent them home with boxed dinners.

"Are you worried about the dig tomorrow?" he asked Layla.

She snuggled closer to him. "Sort of. I want to make sure my students stay safe."

"They will. I'm glad Gramma Mel insisted everyone stay at the main house. She has plenty of room and loves all the company."

"I'm glad she made the offer. Without the university footing the bill, my students couldn't afford to stay at the hotel any longer. But there's plenty of room here," she said, smiling.

"No way anyone is staying at the party house but us. This is our special place. I like coming here every night." No matter how late he worked out on the ranch, he liked coming back here to Layla. Before he parked his truck he would hear her playing her harmonica and the sound would lure him to her. He didn't want to think about how involved they were getting.

Layla lifted her head and looked up at him. "Has your grandmother asked you anything about us?"

He smiled. "She didn't have to. I think it's pretty obvious we have something going on. She's fine with it. We're adults."

What Gavin decided not to say was that his grandmother hadn't needed to ask anything because he'd told her his true feelings for Layla—and about his doubts that it would go anywhere long-term. Needless to say Gramma Mel hadn't been surprised.

"Besides, she has her hands full with Caldwell now that she's back. They've been apart for a week."

Layla lifted an arched brow. "Caldwell?"

Gavin smiled. "Yes, Caldwell. Don't tell me you haven't picked up on what's between them."

Layla shook her head. "No, I hadn't. But you have?"

"Yes, for years. He's a widower and she's a widow. Never understood why they preferred being so discreet. I guess they like their privacy.

"Since the dig starts early in the morning I guess we need to get to sleep," Gavin said, but he wasn't very convincing, even to his own ears.

"Um, I have other ideas," she said, moving on top of him again. "I like riding you."

Gavin grinned. He definitely liked Layla riding him. More than ever, he was convinced the woman was trying to kill him. But he would enjoy every minute until the end.

Hours later, the ringing of his cell phone woke Gavin. He immediately grabbed it when he recognized the ring tone. "Coop?"

"Yeah, Viper, it's me. We couldn't sleep so we thought we'd set a trap."

Gavin sat up in bed as knots tightened in his stomach. Layla had awakened as well and quickly sat up beside him. Drawing in a deep breath, he asked, "And?"

"And I think you need to get here. I've already called the sheriff. We're here at the shack and we got our man."

Sixteen

Gavin made it to the shack in record time, but he wasn't surprised to see several vehicles already there, including the sheriff's. Roy must have been in the area.

With Layla walking quickly by his side, he moved toward the shack but stopped when the door opened and his grandmother stepped out. Her crestfallen features and the tears in her eyes made him pause. *What the hell…?*

He looked past her to Caldwell, who had his grandmother's hand tucked securely in his. The older man shook his head sadly. Gavin felt Layla move closer to his side and he placed his hand in hers.

"I'm taking your grandmother to my place," Caldwell said. "That's where she'll be. You need to go on in now. He's already confessed."

Gavin frowned. *He who? And why was his grandmother crying*? Tightening his grip on Layla's hand, he entered the shack.

Everyone looked up when he and Layla walked in. Roy and Gavin's four SEAL friends. Was he imagining things or were the five looking at him strangely? A funny feeling settled in his gut. Stepping into the room, he glanced around. "Okay, guys. What's going on? Where is he?"

The group shifted and he saw the man seated in a chair with his hands handcuffed behind his back. Gavin shook his head as if to clear his brain. "Mr. Lott?" he said in shock.

Sherman Lott couldn't even look at him. Gavin shook his head again and looked over at his friends. "There must be some mistake. Mr. Lott has been our neighbor for years. He was a friend of Dad's. He—"

"I was never a friend of your father's!" Lott all but screamed. "Gavin Jr. always got anything he wanted. He was the town's hero in high school. I could never compete. Then he became a SEAL and was a war hero, and I couldn't compete there, either. He got all the girls. After my leg got banged up that time when a horse threw me, the women around here wouldn't give me the time of day."

Gavin stared at the man who was now glaring back at him with cold and hate-filled eyes. Gavin let go of Layla's hand. Evidently he had misunderstood this man's relationship with his father all these years. "Okay, so there was a rivalry between you and Dad, and he wasn't your friend. What does that have to do with you sabotaging a dig on my property?"

Instead of answering, Lott shifted his gaze from Gavin to Layla. "I removed that marker so you'd forget where you were supposed to dig, but that didn't stop you. I burned that damn barn down and that didn't stop you, either. You were determined to dig anyway."

"Why didn't you want her to dig, Mr. Lott?" Gavin asked.

The man didn't answer. He looked away as if ignoring the question.

Gavin looked over at his friends. "Would any of you care to explain just what the hell is going on? Why didn't Lott want Layla's team to dig up buried treasure?"

Roy cleared his throat and said in a somber voice, "It wasn't the buried treasure he was concerned with anyone finding, Gavin."

Gavin frowned. Now he was even more confused. "Then what was it?"

The room quieted and he felt Layla pressing her body closer to his. Then she again placed her hand in his. When no one answered, Lott hollered out, "Your mother! I didn't want you to find your mother's body."

Layla felt weak in the knees and wondered how Gavin could still be standing. His friends evidently wondered the same thing as Bane and Coop crossed the room to flank Gavin's other side. Suddenly, she realized they hadn't done so to keep Gavin steady on his feet. They'd moved to intercede if Gavin took a mind to kill Sherman Lott.

"You refused an attorney, Mr. Lott," Roy said angrily. "Like I told you before, any confession you make will hold up in court."

Layla saw Flipper hold up his phone, letting everyone know he was recording everything. Gavin moved forward, and she, Bane and Coop fell in step. It was apparent the shock of what Lott had said had worn off.

"What do you mean 'my mother's body'?" Gavin asked, standing less than five feet from Lott.

Layla thought she actually saw regret fill Mr. Lott's eyes when he said, "I didn't mean to kill her. Honest. It was an accident."

Gavin drew in a breath so deep, it seemed the room rattled from the effect. She felt it. She thought everybody in the room felt it. "You killed my mother?" he asked in an incredulous voice. "But how? She left here."

The man shook his head. "No, she didn't. She never left. I came across her one day with a flat tire. Said she'd planned on going away for a while but changed her mind and turned around before even making it to town. She missed you and your dad too much to go anywhere. She was on her way back home. Had made it to the main road to the Silver Spurs when her tire went flat. I offered to help. She was pretty. She smelled good. I thought she was too good for your dad. He didn't deserve her. What man would leave a young wife who looked like her all alone to go play soldier?"

The man paused. "I told her as much. I must have made her nervous by what I said. By the way I was looking at her and all. And then I don't know what happened but I tried to touch her. She slapped me and I got mad. I slapped her back. I admit to hitting her several more times. She managed to get away and she ran from me. That made me angry. I ran after her and she fell and hit her head."

"And you didn't go get help?" Gavin asked in a voice that was as hard as steel.

"No!" Lott snapped. "Too late. Blood was everywhere. I knew she was dead. Besides, had she lived she would have told everyone what I tried to do. So I dug a hole and buried her."

Layla could almost see steam coming out of Gavin's ears. He was breathing deeply. The hand holding hers tightened in fury.

"What about the car?" Roy asked. Maybe the sheriff figured the best thing to do was keep the conversation going. Otherwise the deathly silence might put crazy ideas into Gavin's head. Like crossing the room and breaking Sherman Lott's neck with his bare hands.

"I drove the car into my lake," Lott said.

"You bastard!" Gavin roared. He would have moved closer but Bane and Coop blocked him. "You buried my mother in a hole not knowing if she was alive or dead? And then you drove her car into the lake?"

Lott had the nerve to glare at Gavin. "Why do you think I wouldn't let anyone swim or fish in my lake? Why I kept it off-limits to you or anyone? Especially to you. I knew how well you could swim and figured one day you might dive too far down and see the car."

Layla saw fierce rage on Gavin's face and she felt it in his entire body. The thought of him being *that* enraged scared her. She glanced over at Bane and Coop. They looked just as enraged as Gavin.

Coop then said in a menacingly calm voice, speaking directly to Gavin but not taking his eyes off Lott. "Now you know why he tried keeping anyone from digging in the south pasture, Viper. Let Roy take him in."

"No!" Gavin roared. "That bastard killed my mother."

"We know," Bane said in a chilling tone, giving Lott one hell of a lethal stare. "We all heard. And although we want to get a damn machete and chop his ass into little pieces, we won't. Let the law take care of him, Viper. In the end he's going to get exactly what he deserves."

The room got quiet and all eyes shifted to Gavin. Even Lott looked petrified upon seeing the deadly glint in Gavin's eyes. There was no doubt in Layla's mind that everyone in that room remembered that, when he needed to be, Gavin Blake could become a killing machine.

Then suddenly Gavin pulled his hand free of hers, shoved both of his hands into the pockets of his jeans and began slowly backing up, not taking his eyes off Lott. It was as if he was trying to pull himself together. As if he knew that staying in that room with Lott one more second meant he would lose control and do the man bodily harm. Gavin kept backing up until his back touched the door. He turned to open it and then stopped. He paused before turning back around.

Layla held her breath, not knowing what Gavin intended to do next. From the tension in the room, she knew his SEAL friends were poised, anticipating his next move. Then his gaze shifted from Lott to her. She saw both pain and anger in his features and her heart hurt for him. The man she loved. She wanted to think he needed her, but would he shut her out of the emotions he was feeling?

The room was deathly still as he continued to stare at her. Then he moved forward...toward her. When he stood right in front of her, he took her hand in his again. Then, without saying a single word, he led her out the door.

Seventeen

Gavin wanted to pull his truck to the side of the road and catch his breath. But he couldn't. Something propelled him to keep driving until he reached the party house. He needed Layla as much as he needed to breathe. She wasn't saying anything. Just sitting in the bench seat beside him and staring straight ahead. It was as if she knew he needed complete silence. His mind was in a state of shock and he was fighting to keep control. Fearful that at any moment he might lose it.

Every time he thought about what Lott had confessed to doing, his mind would spin. Become filled with deadly thoughts and tempt him to turn the truck around and go back to the shack and beat the hell out of the man. How could anyone do what Lott had done and live with himself all these years? And to think no one had suspected a thing until Layla had shown up wanting to dig on their property.

Gavin released a deep breath when he turned into the driveway. Moments later he brought the truck to a stop beside Layla's rental car. Then he was out of the vehicle and moving to the passenger side of the truck. He was there when she opened the door.

Sweeping her into his arms, he headed for the porch, taking the steps two at a time. Grateful that in their rush to leave they'd left the door unlocked, he pushed it open and went inside. Barely taking time to close it behind him, he put Layla on her feet and began ripping off his clothes. She followed his lead and quickly removed hers.

He needed to be inside her. Now.

Taking hold of her waist, he lifted her up and released a throaty growl while pressing her body against the door, spreading her legs wide in the process. Then he was at her entrance, filled with an adrenaline high so potent he could feel blood rushing through his veins, especially the thick ones at the head of his shaft. Desire, as intense as it could get, became a throbbing need pulsating within him.

He thrust hard into her. Over and over again. Needing the release that only her body could give him. Leaning in, he captured her lips with his as sensations, too overpowering to be controlled, rammed through him. When she wrapped her legs around him, she propelled him to make his strokes harder and longer.

Their kiss was so sexually charged he wasn't sure how much longer he could last. He was being robbed of any logical thought except becoming a part of this woman's body. This woman, who had come to mean so much to him. This woman, who made him feel things he'd never felt before with anyone else.

And when she tore her mouth away from his just seconds before her body detonated, her spiraling climax triggered his own and he stroked her with hard and steady thrusts. He hollered her name, drowning in emotions so powerful they seemed to rock his world. A world that a short while ago had been torn apart. He couldn't stop his heart from racing at the magnitude of what he felt. At the magnitude of all he desired.

He knew then that if he'd had any doubt before regarding what Layla had come to mean to him, there was none now.

"Sorry. I should not have taken you that way. But I needed you so damn much, Layla."

They lay together in bed. After making love against the door, Gavin had picked her up and carried her into the bedroom. Then they'd slid beneath the covers and he had held her. She had held him. Layla knew that sleep wasn't an option.

She snuggled closer, needing his heat. Needing a reminder of how much she had been desired. "No apology needed. I liked it."

"I was rough."

"You were good as usual." He had needed her, just like he'd said. Layla had felt that need with every stroke.

"I lost control," he admitted in a low voice. "That's never happened to me before. Hell, Layla, I didn't even take time to put on a condom."

She'd noticed. Had exhilarated in the feeling of being skin to skin with him. Had loved the moment he had blasted off inside of her. The feel of his hot release had felt so right. How could she tell him that? But she knew she had to.

She lifted her face from his chest, met the dark eyes staring down at her. "I liked the feel of you inside me without a condom, Gavin. And don't worry about me getting pregnant. Although I was never sexually active, I decided to get the birth control implant anyway. Better to be safe than sorry. I didn't have to think about it, not like the pill where you have to remember to take one every day." She paused. "And I'm healthy so you don't have to worry about me giving you anything."

He shifted their positions in bed, slipping his arms around her and holding her close. "I'm healthy, too, and you don't have to worry about me giving you anything, either."

He then cupped her chin. "Although I didn't like being rough with you, I enjoyed making love to you without a condom, too."

And then he didn't say anything and she didn't, either. She figured he needed the silence. But when it stretched for what she thought was too long, she moved to lie on top of him and stared into the face she loved so much.

"Talk to me, Gavin. Tell me what you're feeling."

A part of her wondered what right she had to stick her nose into his business, to assume he wanted to tell her anything. But another part of her knew she couldn't let him withdraw. Just like he'd needed her physically, she wanted him to need her emotionally, as well.

She knew his eyes well. Just as well as she knew the shape of his mouth and the fullness of those lips that had kissed her earlier. He would try to fight her on this but she wouldn't let him. He'd been by himself this way for so long she figured it was hard for him to allow another person into his space. Especially a woman. But she had news for him. She wasn't just any woman. She was the woman who loved him.

And for some reason, although he'd never given her reason to say the words, a part of her believed he knew how she felt. A part of her wanted to believe that he knew she wouldn't share her body with just anyone. This wasn't just an excavation fling for her. It was more. But maybe he didn't know. Men had a tendency to be dense when it came to the I-love-you stuff.

"For a minute I felt like a loose cannon, Layla," he said, interrupting her thoughts. "So out of control. I could have snapped and killed Lott with my bare hands. It would have given me pleasure to hear the sound of his neck breaking."

His words, spoken with deep emotion, invaded her mind. She had felt his anger and she'd seen how he'd managed to hold it in check after hearing everything the man had said. Of course the sheriff had been there to stop Gavin from taking matters into his own hands. And his SEAL teammates had been there, too, although she wasn't sure if they would have stopped him or helped him.

"But now you know the truth, Gavin. Your mother never left you and your dad, after all. She's been here all this time. Here on the Silver Spurs."

She watched his eyes flash with confusion. She explained further. "You remember when you told me how the south pasture was your favorite area and your father's, as well. How the two of you would often camp out there. How you loved the feel of sleeping under the stars?"

"Yes."

"I want to think that although the two of you didn't know it, the reason that area meant so much was because your mom was there. She was *there*, Gavin, and when you were there, without knowing it, you were close to her."

She saw the moment when her words sank in. Something broke within him. His eyes might not have been expressive to others but they were expressive to her. Without saying anything, he cupped the back of her neck and brought her mouth down to his. Their tongues tangled in a mating so intense that when he finally released her mouth, she felt light-headed and breathless.

Layla was glad she had given him something to think about. But she knew he must still feel guilty over what he'd believed all these years— that his mother had deserted him and his father. His next words proved her right.

"But I didn't know, Layla. I thought she had gone. I thought she was living another life some- where without us. I thought—"

She placed a finger to his lips. "What you

thought was understandable. You were only a child when she disappeared. But your dad knew his wife. He knew their love. He always believed she would come back. And she did. In fact, she never left. She's been here for the two of you the entire time. And I know she was proud of your dad and was just as proud of you. The man you've become."

He pulled her close, buried his face in her neck. And she held him. Held him tight and near her heart. A part of her wanted to tell him now how much she loved him, but she knew it wasn't the time. That admission would come later. For now this was what he needed. To know she was here and that he wasn't alone.

Bane's ringtone woke Gavin and he glanced out the window as he sat up. It was daybreak. "Yes, Bane?" He nodded. "We're on our way."

When he clicked off the phone, he said, "Let's get dressed. Both your team and mine are ready. Now they have two treasures to find."

A short while later, Gavin pulled his truck to a stop in front of what Layla knew should have been the excavation site. Instead it resembled a crime scene with yellow tape marking the area. Upon hearing the sound of the truck, everyone turned their way. A blanket of snow covered the hillside and forecasters predicted even heavier snow by the weekend. They would need to work quickly.

Layla saw her students standing in a huddle. They'd probably heard what was going on and were trying to figure out how they'd slept through it all. She also saw Ms. Melody standing close to Caldwell, the man's arms wrapped protectively around her. Nothing discreet there. If anyone hadn't realized they were a couple before, they sure knew it now.

Roy was talking on the phone and Gavin's teammates stood next to the digging equipment. She wondered if they'd gotten any sleep, although they looked wide-awake and ready for any action that might come their way.

She'd been so busy observing everyone that she'd failed to notice that Gavin had gotten out of the truck until he was opening the passenger door. He leaned over her to unsnap her seat belt and then effortlessly lifted her out of her seat. "Thanks," she said, when he'd placed her on her feet.

"Don't mention it."

Taking her hand, he walked to where the others were standing. His grandmother left her place by Caldwell's side and walked over to Gavin. He released his hold on Layla's hand and pulled Ms. Melody into a big hug. Giving the two some privacy, Layla joined her students. She figured they would have a lot of questions.

After talking to her team, she returned to Gavin and his teammates. Coop explained how they'd fingered Sherman Lott as the bad guy. "After you told us about the footprint and how it was apparent more pressure was being placed on one foot than the other, we knew we were looking for someone with a leg injury or some kind of impairment and who was wearing worn shoes. When we saw Lott's shoes and saw him rubbing his leg more than once, I got suspicious. I offered him my chair so he wouldn't have to stand. I told him that I noticed his leg seemed to be bothering him. That's when he said it occasionally did and was the result of a horse riding accident years ago."

Coop then nodded for Bane to continue.

"Last night after everyone had gone to bed,"

Bane said, taking up the tale. "Mac and I decided to go to Lott's ranch and snoop around, to see if we could find the kerosene can. Imagine our surprise when we got there and saw him loading up a kerosene can onto his truck, with plans to head back over to your place to burn down the shack. We called Coop and told him to contact you and to call the sheriff. Lott was caught red-handed about to pour kerosene around the shack to torch it."

Roy approached with an angry look on his face. "What's wrong, Roy?" Gavin asked.

"One of the disadvantages of a small town is not having manpower when you need it," Roy said, drawing in a deep breath. "I talked to the sheriff in Palmdale and he said it would be four to five days before their dive team could get here."

Gavin nodded as if he wasn't concerned with that news. "Is there any reason we can't start digging?" he asked.

Roy frowned. "Yes, there's a reason. This is a crime scene."

Gavin shook his head. "Technically it's not. Although I believe everything Lott said, until I find my mother's body there's no proof a crime has been committed. Besides, I'd rather be the one to find her, Roy. And those students over there are entitled to their treasure hunt."

Roy didn't say anything for a minute and then nodded. "Okay, but I will stay here to help and step in if any evidence is found."

"Absolutely," Gavin assured him.

Roy drew in a deep breath and ordered one of his deputies to remove the yellow crime scene tape.

Less than an hour later, the remains of Jamie Blake were found. And within twenty feet of where she'd been buried, a strongbox filled with gold pieces—Jesse James's loot—was also recovered.

Deciding not to wait on the dive team from Palmdale, Flipper had jumped into Lott's lake without any diving gear. When he hadn't resurfaced in five minutes, Roy became worried. Gavin and his other teammates had not. They explained that although the water was icy cold and Flipper had been under longer than normal, Flipper was far from ordinary. They were proven right when a short while later Flipper resurfaced with the license plate he had removed from the car. The license plate was identified as that registered to Gavin and Jamie Blake.

The charges against Sherman Lott were changed from suspicion of murder to murder.

Eighteen

Layla stood at the window. It was snowing and what had begun that morning as small flakes was now huge and covering the earth in a white blanket. Four days had passed since the dig, and activities on the Silver Spurs were returning to normal. Once Gavin's mother's remains had been unearthed, the town's coroner had been called and the yellow tape had been reerected. But not before Jesse James's strongbox filled with gold bars had been uncovered.

The Silver Spurs became the focus of two big news stories—a decades-old murder and the first recorded discovery of Jesse James's loot in the state of Missouri. No-trespassing signs had been posted when the media had converged on the ranch.

Gavin had given his one and only statement regarding the recovery of his mother's remains. "I am glad the truth about my mother's disappearance was discovered and I hope Sherman Lott rots in hell."

A news conference had been held regarding the discovery of Jesse James's loot, which was making international news. Dr. Clayburn arrived in town and tried to claim the university was associated with the dig. Layla refuted his statement since she had documentation in the form of an email from both Dr. Clayburn and the president of the university advising of her termination prior to the dig. The following day, the two men were in even more hot water when photographs surfaced of the two of them involved in illicit affairs with female students. Not surprisingly, Tammy was in many of the photographs, arriving and leaving various hotels with both men.

Layla didn't have to guess where the photographs had come from. Apparently Donnell and some of the other students had exposed the sordid activities. Within twenty-four hours of the photographs being splashed across the front page of the *Seattle Times* and making the national news, the two men, along with a few other faculty members, had turned in their resignations.

Donnell, Wendy and Marsha had joined Layla at the news conference and were acknowledged for their participation on the dig. The Missouri Archaeological Society had authenticated the loot as that stolen by Jesse James from the Tinsel Bank.

Already offers of employment from numerous universities had arrived for Layla, in addition to offers of book deals and television interviews. Yesterday she'd received a call from her grandmother and one from her parents. She had been surprised when her parents told her how proud they were of her. They'd even said she'd done the right thing by following her own dream and not theirs. They invited her to spend the holidays with them in DC.

She drew in a deep breath and moved away from the window to sit on the bed she'd just left a few moments earlier. She had awakened to find Gavin gone. He must have left to check on the ranch with his men. Even with the no-trespassing signs clearly posted, a couple of reporters and their camera crews had encroached on the property only to have Gavin's men run them off again.

The coroner had released his mother's remains and yesterday morning a private memorial service had been held. Jamie Blake had been reburied beside her husband in the family cemetery. Layla had stood beside Gavin along with his grandmother, Caldwell and Gavin's teammates. Even his commanding officer had flown in to attend the service.

After dinner, Gavin's teammates left to return to their various homes, but not before each one had given her a huge hug and told her how glad they'd been to meet her. She had gotten to know the four well and could see why they and Gavin shared such close relationships. Bane, Coop, Flipper and Mac were swell guys who were fiercely loyal to each other. She couldn't thank them enough for their part in recovering Jesse James's loot.

Now that the dig was over, Layla could feel Gavin withdrawing from her. She had tried ignoring it but she knew something was bothering him. She thought it was related to his mother but, to be totally honest, she wasn't sure.

There was no reason for her to remain on the ranch any longer and she had mentioned that she would be leaving in a couple of days to return to Seattle. She had hoped he would ask her to stay but he hadn't. Instead he'd merely nodded and hadn't said anything else about it. Was that his way of letting her know she had outstayed her welcome?

The thought that he wanted her to leave his ranch had tears welling up in her eyes. She'd known when she fell in love with him that there was a big chance he wouldn't love her back. So why was the thought that he didn't breaking her heart?

The time they had spent together on the Silver Spurs had been special but now she had to move on.

Gavin placed his coffee cup on the table, stared at his grandmother and then asked, "What did you just say?"

Melody Blake smiled brightly. "You heard me right, Gavin. Caldwell asked me to marry him. This was his third time asking and I finally said yes. We don't want to make a big fuss about it and Reverend Pollock agreed to perform the ceremony next weekend. I'll be moving into Caldwell's place afterward."

Gavin didn't say anything for a long moment. He was happy for his grandmother and Caldwell. It was about time. "Congratulations. I'm happy for you, Gramma Mel. Caldwell is a good man and I believe the two of you will be happy together."

"Thank you. What about you? What are your plans regarding Layla?"

He lifted his coffee cup and took a sip before saying, "What makes you think I have any?"

His grandmother frowned. "Don't try pretending with me, Gavin Timothy Blake III. You love Layla. You've admitted as much. I would think you'd want to take the next step."

Yes, he had admitted it to her and he didn't regret doing so. "Sometimes taking the next step isn't always possible."

"Why not? I'd think you'd want something permanent between the two of you."

He shook his head. "Layla and I are very different. Dad took Mom out of a big city and brought her here and she was miserable. Layla is from Seattle. She'd be just as unhappy and miserable here as Mom was."

"Have you talked to Layla about it? Have you asked her how she feels?"

"No."

"Then maybe you should. You're basing your opinions on assumptions. I know for a fact Layla loves the Silver Spurs. She said as much."

"But that doesn't mean she loves me. If she doesn't love me, then there's nothing to hold her here. She's gotten a lot of job offers from a number of big universities, including Harvard. All we have in Cornerstone is a small college. Why would she settle for that?"

"Well, I think you'll be making a big mistake if you don't talk to her about it, tell her how you feel. Let her decide what she wants to do. You might discover that she loves you as much as you love her."

An hour or so later, Gavin entered the party house. He removed his hat and shook off the snow from his jacket before hanging both items on the rack.

The first thing he noticed as he headed for the kitchen was that the curtains were still closed. Everything was just as he'd left it at daybreak, which meant Layla hadn't gotten up yet. Placing the box containing the breakfast his grandmother had prepared on the table, he moved down the hallway to the bedroom. Opening the door, he stuck his head inside and saw Layla curled up in bed still sleeping.

The bad weather had pretty much dictated that everyone stay inside. He knew his men had a card game going and he could certainly join them. But he much preferred staying here and joining Layla, right in that bed. What if Gramma Mel was right? What if Layla wanted to stay on the Silver Spurs with him? Would it be fair to ask her to stay when a call from his commanding officer meant he would drop everything for a covert operation? Would she want that?

He sat in a chair and removed his shoes and socks before standing to take off the rest of his clothes. No matter the temperature, he preferred sleeping in the nude, something he couldn't do while away on missions.

Crossing the room, Gavin slid into bed with Layla and pulled her into his arms, to warm his body as well as his heart.

Layla thought she was dreaming when she felt a hot and husky whisper against her ear. It took a moment to open her eyes and gaze into a pair of sexy dark ones staring back at her. Gavin's body was pressed close to hers. It was warm, even hot in certain places, and she knew without a doubt that he was naked.

"We need to talk, Layla."

She heard the seriousness in his voice. Why did they need to talk? He was ready for her to leave. She got that. But why was he rushing her away? Did he already have another woman lined up to share his bed? The thought made her mad and she buried her face in the pillow, but not before saying, "I don't want to talk. I have nothing to say to you."

He pulled the pillow away from her, frowning. "What the hell did I do?"

"Just being a typical man. You share a bed with

a woman, and then you tire of her and want her gone so you can replace her with another."

He stared at her. "You think I would do that?"

"Why wouldn't you? You're a man, aren't you? You're not tied to any woman, especially not to me. It's not like I didn't notice that reporter flirting with you."

He frowned. "What reporter?"

Layla rolled her eyes. "The one that kept putting that microphone all in your face and kept touching your shoulders every chance she got, even when she didn't have to." Layla hated that she'd said something about that. Now she sounded like a jealous hag. Just because they'd slept together a few times didn't mean she had dibs on him.

Before she could catch her next breath, he had flipped her on her back. He loomed over her and held her hands in a tight grip above her head.

"Why would I want another woman, Layla?"

That was really a silly question. "Why wouldn't you want another one?"

He stared down at her with an intensity that made a rush of desire claw through her insides. "Because you are all the woman I need. Hell, I can barely keep up with you, Layla."

* * *

Lord knows that's the truth, Gavin thought, as he felt familiar need hammer through him. Only Layla could do this to him. Make him feel so consumed with desire for her, he would go up in flames. More than once his teammates had told him to take a cold shower when just looking at Layla heated an entire room.

Gavin just stared down at her. She was wearing a nightgown, but barely. It was made of flimsy material and part of it was bunched up around her waist, leaving her bare below. Her hair was loose and tousled around her shoulders. Because of the way he was holding her hands, her breasts jutted up, firm and hard. He could see the impression of rigid nipples through the thin material of her gown.

Just that quickly, her breathing changed. He heard it and then he felt the sinfully erotic movement of her hips against him. After all the times they'd made love right here in this bed, not to mention the times they hadn't made it to the bed, didn't she know how much he wanted her? Her and no other woman? She actually thought she had a reason to be jealous of some damn reporter who couldn't keep her hands to herself?

He knew from the eyes staring back at him that his grandmother was right. Layla had no idea how he felt about her. The woman hadn't a clue. He had told her they needed to talk, and then she'd gone on the offensive. Why? Had his grandmother been right on both accounts, that Layla cared for him as much as he cared for her?

There was only one way to find out.

"Let's backtrack for a minute, Layla. Earlier I asked you why I would want another woman, and you asked why I wouldn't want one. I don't think I made myself clear enough. The main reason I don't want another woman is because I love you. I've fallen in love with you, Layla, and when a man falls in love with one woman she takes away his desire for other women. She becomes the one and only woman he wants in his life, his bed, his home, his mind and his heart. You are that woman for me."

She stared at him for a long time without saying anything. And then he saw it, the tears forming in her eyes. "But if you love me, why were you sending me away?"

He frowned. "I wasn't sending you away. The other night you told me you were going. What was I supposed to do, tell you that you couldn't go?"

She frowned back at him. "You could have told me you loved me."

"Why would I tell you that when I didn't know how you felt? Hell, I still don't know. With your credentials, you can teach anywhere. I know about all those job offers that have come in. Why would you want to stay here? My mother hated it here."

"I love you, too, Gavin, and I love it here. I fell in love with the Silver Spurs the minute I drove onto the land. There are times when I will leave to do speaking engagements and interviews. Maybe even teach a class or two for a semester. However, I will come back. You leave, don't you? To go on your covert operations. Yet you come back. You return and step into your role of a rancher. Why can't I return and step into a similar role."

"As a rancher's wife?"

She lifted her brow. "Wife?"

He smiled down at her. "Yes, wife. You don't

think you'll hang around as my live-in lover, do you? I want to marry you. I want you to one day have my children. I want you to live here on this ranch with me."

"And be here whenever the rancher returns?"

He chuckled. "That would be nice."

A smile touched her lips. "That can be arranged." She didn't say anything for a minute. "About all those offers. I don't want to decide on anything just yet. After dealing with the likes of Clayburn and Connors, I just want to chill for a minute. Possibly write a book. I'd love to take my time and do it here."

He nodded. He needed to let her know something.

Layla waited for him to speak.

"Gramma Mel told me this morning that she and Caldwell are getting married. She's moving to his place. That means you'll be here by yourself whenever I'm away. I'm supposed to report back for duty at the end of January."

"I'll be okay. I will have enough to keep me busy."

Layla wouldn't tell him yet that she wanted lots

of children. She'd always wished for siblings and would make sure she had more than one child. And she didn't want to wait a long time before she began having them.

Before Gavin, she'd never thought beyond her career goals. But now she'd achieved those. With him by her side, she could have everything—success and a family and the man she loved.

"So, will you marry me?"

That question, as far as she was concerned, was a no-brainer. "Yes, Gavin, I will marry you."

He released her hands as he lowered his mouth to hers. She wrapped her arms around his muscled back.

She loved her SEAL, her rancher. For them, the best was yet to come.

Epilogue

Layla couldn't help but dab at her eyes. The vow renewal ceremony for Bane and his wife, Crystal, was simply beautiful. The words they spoke to each other in the presence of family and friends were filled with so much love that Layla couldn't help but shed tears.

Gavin had told her how Bane and Crystal had eloped as teens, and then had been separated for five years when her family had sent her away. But what Layla found so precious was how their love had survived. They had reunited a year ago and since no family members had been present for their first wedding, they'd decided to renew their vows in front of everyone.

What was doubly special was that Crystal and Bane had announced to everyone earlier that day that they were expecting a baby. Everyone could tell from the smiles on the couple's faces that a baby was something they both wanted. Gavin and the guys couldn't wait to tease Bane about impending fatherhood. Mac, who had a number of kids of his own, said he would give Bane pointers on changing diapers.

Today was officially the couple's sixth wedding anniversary and Crystal's twenty-fourth birthday. Layla thought it refreshing to find someone even younger than her with a PhD; they had a lot in common. Crystal was beautiful and Layla thought she was just the woman for Bane.

It was a lovely November day in the city of Denver. And since one of Bane's brother's had married an event planner, the home belonging to Bane's older brother Dillon, where the ceremony took place, had been decorated beautifully in colors of blue and gold. Layla had already talked to Alpha Westmoreland about planning Layla's dream wedding, which would take place in June.

"You okay, baby?" Gavin whispered before

boldly using his tongue to lick away one of her tears.

"Behave, Gavin," she whispered back in a warning tone, knowing when it came to her he wouldn't behave.

She glanced around to see if anyone had noticed what he'd done. Bane certainly had a big family. There were Westmorelands everywhere. Gavin had warned her but she hadn't believed him. No wonder the locals referred to this section of Denver as Westmoreland Country. There were also some Westmorelands who lived in Atlanta, Montana and Texas. She'd even discovered Bane's cousin was married to a king in a country in the Middle East. All the Westmorelands she'd met were friendly and made her feel so welcome.

Another couple she'd met and liked right away was Bane's cousin Bailey and her husband, Walker Rafferty. They lived in Alaska. Layla hadn't wanted to keep staring at Walker but she remembered when he'd been a movie star years ago. He'd been a heartthrob then and he was definitely one today. She recalled seeing his picture on the cover of a recent issue of *Simply Irresist-*

ible magazine. When she'd mentioned it to Bailey, the woman had chuckled and looked up at her husband adoringly before saying, "There's a story behind that. One day I will have to tell you about it."

It was good seeing Gavin's teammates again. Layla was glad to meet Mac's wife, Teri. The mother of four was simply gorgeous. Everyone planned to visit the Silver Spurs in June for Gavin and Layla's wedding. They'd agreed to spend Thanksgiving at the ranch and Christmas with her family. Ms. Melody and Caldwell had married and seemed to be very happy together.

Layla looked down at her engagement ring. It was beautiful. They had talked about Gavin giving Layla his mother's wedding set. Jamie had still been wearing the rings when her body had been unearthed. But Gavin had said he wanted Layla to have her own special rings and he would keep the rings his father had given his mother to pass on to their first son... Gavin Blake IV. She smiled at the audacity of Gavin thinking he would one day have a son to carry on the Blake name.

When the minister told Bane he could kiss his

wife, everyone cheered. Bane pulled Crystal into his arms and gave her one hell of a kiss. What the couple shared was definitely special. Just as special as what Layla and Gavin shared.

Bane then leaned over and whispered something in Crystal's ear, which made her blush. Layla leaned over to Gavin. "I guess you heard that." He had told her about what his teammates dubbed as his sonic ears.

Gavin smiled. "Yes, I heard. Every single naughty word."

"The ceremony was beautiful," Layla said, fighting back more tears.

Gavin took her hand, brought it to his lips and kissed her knuckles. "And so are you. I can't wait until the day you will officially have my name."

Layla couldn't wait, either. He'd been trying to talk her into eloping in January and having a huge wedding reception in June. He wanted them to be married before he left for this next covert operation. She was giving his suggestion some serious thought.

"And I can't wait until later, when I get you back to our hotel room," he added, whispering close to her ear.

Layla smiled as they linked hands and walked out of the church. She knew her life with her SEAL/rancher would never be boring.

* * * * *

MILLS & BOON®

Why shop at millsandboon.co.uk?

Each year, thousands of romance readers find their perfect read at millsandboon.co.uk. That's because we're passionate about bringing you the very best romantic fiction. Here are some of the advantages of shopping at www.millsandboon.co.uk:

* **Get new books first**—you'll be able to buy your favourite books one month before they hit the shops

* **Get exclusive discounts**—you'll also be able to buy our specially created monthly collections, with up to 50% off the RRP

* **Find your favourite authors**—latest news, interviews and new releases for all your favourite authors and series on our website, plus ideas for what to try next

* **Join in**—once you've bought your favourite books, don't forget to register with us to rate, review and join in the discussions

Visit **www.millsandboon.co.uk**
for all this and more today!